THE PURR-FECT SOLDIER

VIVIENNE SAVAGE

THE PURR-FECT SOLDIER

WILD OPERATIVES #3

By Vivienne Savage

http://www.viviennesavage.com

1

TAYLOR

*W*hen put to the vote, wrestling always won over any other television program.

I rolled my eyes and went with the flow, settling on the bench with a bowl of ramen, squeeze cheese, and diced summer sausage in my lap. It was Mack's secret recipe, a damned delicacy in this place. I only trusted it because I watched him make the shit.

One of the guys changed the channel just in time for the starting chatter about how some wrestler was going to beat some other guy's ass. The announcement was made in the classic series of threats and bravado. They screamed at each other at the top of their lungs, made aggressive gestures, and then the announcer took over.

"Sup, Taylor? I heard you gettin' out soon."

I glanced toward my right. A beefy guy with a chest like a gorilla sat beside me. He wore his hair trimmed low on top, bald at the sides and back. Upraised prison tats went up and down his arms in black ink like pigmented scar tissue — the sign of a shitty job done with a hypodermic needle and ink from a BIC pen.

"Sup, Slick. Yeah, I am. About fucking time, too."

"Parole?"

I nodded.

"Damn. You know we got that thing coming up. We could use you, bro."

"I don't wanna fuck up my chance at parole, dawg. Sorry." Getting mixed up in a riot was the last thing I wanted or needed.

"Yeah, you right. You right. Besides, the Deuce wanted me to let you know he needs to have a word with you. You gotta meet him tomorrow during rec."

I nodded again. "Sure thing. Morning or evening?"

"Evening."

At the end of the night, long after the wrestling program ended, the doors opened and a guard in a starched, gray suit entered the room. Lights out. We were all shuffled one row at a time to our cells like cattle. The doors rolled open, we stepped in, and they shut behind us.

I shared a cell with a big white guy called Mack, aptly named for his physical resemblance to a Mack truck. He and my werebear friend Russ had something in common, with muscles bulging off their muscles.

"Yo, Tay, I can still have all your stuff when you go, right?"

"Yeah. Do I look like I wanna take twenty bucks worth of noodles with me into the free world?"

I tossed my prison whites aside to be washed the next day then crawled into the top bunk. With my eyes closed, I imagined the feel of the grass beneath my paws. The fresh air against my fur, whistling over my ears. Anything beat the stench of the prison and a couple thousand men in a hot box.

One more week and I could punch Ian in his damned face for suggesting the stupid idea of sending me undercover into a nearby penitentiary. Ferguson Unit had been my home since late March, and if I didn't love him like a brother, I'd probably pluck all his feathers once I got out. All this time, six months, and I wasn't anywhere close to digging up the info he wanted. All I'd found out was that a con named 'the Deuce' had a street thug named Dennis killed. Dennis was the baby daddy of Ian's new wife. She had dated the guy before his criminal behavior got him put away for twenty-five years. But that was another story.

"Bitch, turn the fucking lights off!" someone screamed from his cell at the poor officer busting her behind to keep ahead. My months of incarceration fostered a new respect for working women. I used to think girls like my female squad mates, Sasha and Juni, were the only ones who had it hard. Then I met these women. The officer yelled something back, and fifteen minutes later, the overhead cell block lights dimmed.

Eventually, a voice on the loudspeaker announced count time. I watched her go by with her sheet of paper and flashlight, a curvy figure in stiff grays with abundant brown curls fastened into a bun.

I can't wait to get out of here and get laid. How the hell do these men manage this for years?

I watched her pass by a second time, sighed, and rolled over to go to sleep. The monotony of day-to-day life began at three a.m. when we were roused for breakfast. I choked down overcooked scrambled eggs and eventually reported in for my job as the warden's personal janitor.

I had Ian to thank for it as much as I had him to blame for being in prison in the first place. He pulled strings, got me put where he needed me to be, and, in return, I reported shit to the prison officials. I was playing both sides, leaking info to make friends with inmates and tipping off the prison administration.

By evening, I had nervous jitters.

What the hell did this guy want with me? I couldn't have offended him. As the unchallenged leader of the prison minorities, the Deuce had enough pull to get guys in my cell at night if he wanted. It only took one crooked officer to make it happen. And if they resorted to that, I'd have no choice but to shapeshift and take them out. I'd explain the claw and teeth marks later.

I shuffled down a corridor, nearly a half mile long, following a train of men with the same destination. Hard cement covered every inch of the floor, echoing loud voices surrounding us. A stressed guard watched us with his hand on his can of pepper spray, his face like a bulldog's, the smell of a hard day clinging to his sweat-drenched body.

The prison's main areas sweltered during the summers. Air conditioning was a gift granted only to the administrative offices and infirmary. Officers and felons alike suffered in misery.

I reached the end of the line where a trio of male officers waited with cheap exam gloves on their hands.

"All right. Come out of 'em," one demanded.

I bit my tongue and complied, removing my clothes and handing each article over one at a time.

It's not like I gave a damn about doing their naked dance in the hallway. It was the principle of it. Once prison guards finished strip-searching the group of us lined up for recreation, I was free to go. Pulling my shirt on again, I strode onto the grass, relieved by the caress of the evening breeze against my face. The fresh air rustled my sweat-dampened prison whites and carried the grassy scent of the pastures to me from the nearby field.

I sought the Deuce out and found the big man pumping iron at the weight machines. He had about fifty pounds on me, built like a freight train — hardly unusual since most guys had nothing better to do than work out excessively.

"Sup, man. Slick said you wanted to talk."

The Deuce passed the weight bar to his spotter and sat up, panting heavily. Sweat glistened on his dark skin, a mix of Hispanic and Black ancestry apparent in his features. "Yeah. I have an opportunity for you. Word around the prison is that you're gonna move local. Stay in the Huntsville area. That right?"

"Yeah. I came from Dallas originally, but I don't have any family left. A friend of a friend assured me I can pick up work easy in this area."

"Your friend's right, if you have the right skills. What you planning on doing?"

"Mechanic. I'm good with cars."

"Well then, I think I can hook you up. When you get out, man, you talk to my boy Tito up in Quick-draw. He runs the garage there."

"Yeah? Thanks, man, I appreciate it."

"You tell Tito I sent you, and maybe pass him a few messages for me."

"Sure thing. Whatever you need." This was it. My chance to get a foot in the door on their outside operations.

"Let him know his problems are—"

I smelled the guy coming from a mile away. The dwindling, evening sun glinted off the shiv swinging toward my back. I ducked and weaved out of the way, pivoting on a foot to face one of our attackers. My fist came up and blocked the assault as another rushed the Deuce from his left. We were outnumbered and the officer on the rec yard had taken that moment to chat with another inmate by the ball court. The boss in the guard tower was probably in the john.

Five of them against two of us. The Deuce was accustomed to prison brawling, but I was the one with the cat-like reflexes. I moved fast, my hands a blur used only to defend myself. I twisted the arm of my primary assailant, forcing him to drop the shiv. Then I kicked the back of his knee in and shoved him face first to the ground. He struck his face on the pavement and was out for the count. His prone sprawl allowed me a glimpse of the blue lightning bolts tatted to the back of his neck.

Gang fight. I'd seen more than a couple since going undercover. The power struggles never stopped.

"Fight!" the officer screamed. Her panicked voice began to rattle off details of the assault over the radio.

I snapped my foot toward another skinhead's face. He had all the markings of a guy in the Aryan Brotherhood, or maybe even the Circle. Hell if I could tell without analyzing his tattoos even closer.

"Holy shit! Look at Tay go!" someone cried. Nobody had seen me fight before, my skills a closely guarded secret until now. I'd only had to hand one dude his ass in the showers back in May, and

Warden Johansen had him transferred off the prison unit after his recovery.

Two left standing. Where the hell is the guard? With one man between me and the Deuce, I couldn't defend him from the guy squaring off against him. He was shanked in the side, once, twice, a third time before the gas grenade exploded to my right.

2

JADA

*T*ranquil music played through the storefront speakers as I sipped a frosty mocha Frappuccino. I waited for my afternoon client, a new mother with a spa day gift card from her doting fiancé.

I envied women like her with their shit together. A career, a good man, and a family—three of the four things my mom claimed every woman needed for success. Of course, Dani had an education, too. She had it all. She had the life I wanted for myself one day.

The clock ticked, only three minutes past four. The storefront of *Nirvana* had a shop counter beside a fifty-five-gallon aquarium of yellow labidochromis fish and cichlids. By the wall, a shelf held rows of shampoo, conditioner, and personal goodies for the clientele to purchase. Behind us, the salon floor held four chairs with mirrors on each side, as well as two shampoo basins and two hood dryers.

The shop was my baby.

With a tote bag on her arm, Daniela Reyes wandered past the storefront window. The door chime sang and announced her entrance, but I was right in front of the door to bounce to my feet and greet her.

"Afternoon, Dani," I chirped. "You ready for this day of pampering?" I aimed a smile at the woman as she stepped through the stained glass doorway. She'd been my first customer when I opened the doors to the spa last year, and she'd been a regular ever since.

"More than ready. I even left my cell phone behind in the car."

"Poor Russ. Forced to make do without calling you every five minutes to ask why the baby's squirming."

We had a good laugh at her husband and headed into the back. I settled Dani in a room for her wax and massage. At first, we worked in silence until the tough part was over. The backrub came last, a necessary treat.

"So, tell me, how is the baby doing?" I asked as I rubbed sweet almond oil into her knotted shoulder muscles. The aroma of eucalyptus and mint essential oils filled the small room from the nearby diffuser.

"Finally sleeping for at least five hours a night. Seven if we're lucky."

"It will get better, I promise. My cousin Padma said things began to settle out with her daughter around four months."

Serene music played as I treated Dani to an hour long massage, working her muscles loose from head to toe. At the end of her time, I settled the sheet over her relaxed body.

"Take as long as you need, Dani. No rush. Catch a nap if you'd like, and I'll see you in the front for your hair."

While my client dozed in privacy, I stepped to the front and smiled at the three women chatting together. Lisa and Naomi worked for me as hairstylists and had their own preferred customers. I had mine.

"Afternoon, Leigh," I greeted her, only to be embraced in an enthusiastic hug. "Back to freshen up your highlights, huh?" Like Daniela, Leigh MacArthur scheduled regular appointments with me, often visiting together.

"Naomi talked me into it," she said. "How's Dani? I saw her car outside."

"Relaxed and snoozing. It was sweet of Russ to buy her a package."

"Yeah, Russ is a teddy bear," Leigh said with a giggle.

A client for Lisa entered as I settled Leigh at my chair. With Daniela asleep, I had time to highlight and trim her friend.

"How's Mr. MacArthur enjoying his new job?"

"He loves it. He claims being sheriff is simpler than being an Air Force colonel."

We both shared a laugh. I'd voted for Ian, too, and my father had been relieved when the man won the election by a landslide.

By the time Daniela emerged from the back, I'd gotten Leigh under the dryer.

"Are you excited about the upcoming graduation?" I asked her.

"Definitely," Dani replied.

"I can't begin to tell you how happy my dad will be to have a bank in town. He hates driving into the city."

Daniela chuckled. "It's going to take a while to get established, but I hope it'll be worth it. Everyone says they'll open an account to support me, but you know how it is."

"Don't I," I groaned. "I'd be generous if I said even

half the people who made promises came in. It was so disappointing."

"It'll happen, Jada. You've got a good place here and a smart business plan."

"Do you really think they'll give me the loan, Dani?"

"Keep this between you and me, but I'm absolutely certain," Daniela said while winking, "you won't have a problem with your approval."

I sagged in relief. "Thank you so much. I can't begin to tell you how grateful I am—"

"Then don't. You've given people a reason to come to Quickdraw over Huntsville. This town needs to grow."

"Quickdraw is home. I couldn't imagine moving anywhere else just to be closer to some big chain store. If we bring the businesses here, people won't have to move." I gestured toward my employees. Lisa, our barber, was busy with one of her male clients. "No one has to drive into the next city to get a job."

When complaints poured in from my customers about the local nail salon, I knew it was an opportunity to move ahead. I wanted to buy the recently vacated shop beside me and renovate it to include mani/pedi work stations.

"It'll all work out, Jada. Trust me."

"You should come out with us when your shift is over," Leigh invited. "We're going to have dinner over at the fondue place that just opened up on Main Street. Cheese, chocolate, and wine."

"I don't want to impose."

"Nonsense." Dani gave a dismissive wave. "The more company the merrier, or so the saying goes. Girls' night out, Jada. It'll be a fun way for you to unwind after a day on your feet. Please?"

Daniela's pleading face and attempt at puppy dog eyes won me over.

Two hours later, I was in the rear seat of Dani's badass car after the girls picked me up from my place. The Perfect Pot had a table waiting for us under a reservation, and soon we had two steaming cheese dips with various veggies and bread bites for dipping.

It was like an extension of our time in the salon, chatter consuming every subject from their school careers to their home lives.

"Did Russ say anything to you about a job?" Leigh suddenly blurted out to our friend.

"No. Is there supposed to be one?" Dani asked in return.

Leigh bit her lower lip. "I don't think so."

"So why are you asking me? You know about as much as I do," Dani assured her. "What happened?"

"Okay, so Ian says they're all done with this stuff, but yesterday some big guy in D.C. called and begged him to go to Palestine to handle some big problem."

I nearly choked on my wine. "Wait, what? Palestine as in the Middle East, not Palestine, Texas, you mean?"

"You know that security company he owns?"

"Yeah, he installed the system at my place. I love it," I replied.

"Well, he also manages private contract work for the military, too," Leigh explained. "Sort of like a mercenary. He stepped back from the business and promoted a close friend to take it over because he wanted to become sheriff."

"And be here for you and Sophia," Dani reminded her.

"Oh, wow. I mean, I had no idea he was Special Forces."

"You know Ian. He hates tooting his own horn." Leigh poured wine in all our glasses. "Of course, I love that about him, and a huge part of me is glad he's not going out as much anymore."

"Russ promises he's done with it all, too, but sometimes I think he's tired of the home life every day. I mean, they're going from nonstop excitement to posing as old men sitting on porches with games of Checkers."

"He's in the volunteer fire department," I pointed out. "He does get some excitement."

"When do they *ever* have anything to do?" Dani asked. She shrugged and dipped a breadstick into the fondue pot.

"Maybe we should go adopt a bunch of kittens from the shelter and put them up in trees." I giggled at my own absurd suggestion. "You know when he came in to get his haircut from Naomi, I overheard him telling her he *likes* being a stay-at-home dad."

Leigh sighed. "Ian says the same thing, but I feel awful leaving him with Sophia all the time when I'm in class."

"You ladies have good men. The last jerk I went out with hated kids." I sighed and pulled over the dessert menu. "How do you even choose one when these all look amazing?"

Leigh leaned over for a peek. "Oooh, turtle fudge."

"You can't go wrong with chocolate peanut butter," Dani said.

We indulged and ordered both of the sweet treats. I dipped marshmallow after marshmallow into a pot of rich chocolate laced with gooey peanut butter. The pieces melted in my mouth, the perfect end to a fabulous evening. I thought they'd have to roll me out of my chair and to Dani's car, but somehow I made it to the backseat.

"I had a great time, ladies. Thanks for inviting me."

Leigh and Dani exchanged mischievous grins. "We're heading down to The Outlets this weekend. Come with us," Dani invited.

"That's almost a three hour drive!" I protested.

"We'll take Ian's SUV and ride in style," Leigh promised as they parked in front of my house.

"I don't know..."

"What else do you have to do?" Dani asked.

After I agreed to accompany them on their wild shopping spree, I stepped up to my porch and unlocked the door.

My humble home was a single-level house with a shoebox-sized front yard, only a five-minute walk up the street from the spa. Before I had the day spa, I took clients off the street and styled hair in the second bedroom, tolerating the cramped quarters as a necessity.

Maybe the floors needed a good sanding and the windows could use new screens, but I couldn't complain when it was all mine. I paid it off before taking on a pile of loans to open my business.

Leaving my shoes on the porch, I stepped inside

and clicked on the living room light. A love seat, modest television, and an aquarium shelf filled the space, leaving no room for anything else. "Did you miss me, girls?" I peeked down into a fish tank at my sorority of female bettas then pinched in a bit of their food. I had a second tank on the shelf above them, home to a single enormous male with a pearlescent body and lavender fins. I'd paid far too much money for him from a breeder two years ago, but I loved him.

My phone rang as I was wiggling out of my bra. I tossed it onto the corner of the couch and flopped into the seat. God, I loved that moment of setting the tatas free after a tiring day. "Hey, Mom," I answered. I put my feet up after tucking the phone between my ear and shoulder, the remote and PlayStation controller on my lap. I signed into Netflix and planned to let the next episode of *Orange is the New Black* drown out my mother.

"So, I have pleasing news for you, Jada."

"Uh huh."

"Hazim's son agreed to meet with you this weekend. Aren't you happy?"

"Yeah."

"You will have to do something with your hair, of course, and visit the store tomorrow to buy something nice to wear. No more of those frumpy clothes you're so fond of buying. That dress you wore to your father's family reunion resembled a potato sack, baby. You must pick something else. Now, he isn't Indian, but what does race matter? Love is love, as your father proves." My mom was Indian, but she'd married a white guy after she immigrated to the U.S. She was pregnant with me at the time, and Dad had raised me like his own child.

"Uh huh."

"Well, what do you think?" Mom asked. "Jada? Is this weekend good for you?"

"No," I replied automatically, absolutely clueless. I hadn't heard a word she said until then, but her tone implied that 'no' was the only correct answer. Last time she had set me up, I'd wanted to claw my egotistical date's eyes out. He'd spent most of the evening checking out every woman we passed.

"You did not even consider my request," she argued.

I didn't need to. My mom lived for one thing, and that was getting grandchildren out of me.

I'm not even thirty. It's not like the expiration stamp on my ovaries was dated for tomorrow, but she behaved like my eggs were already spoiled.

"He is a nice boy. What else are you doing this weekend that's more important than meeting a sweet young man? He will be coming home for good from the military soon, his mother says."

With my finger on the mute button, I groaned out loud. I had nothing against military guys, but if I was going to give up my freedom to date, I'd rather it be with someone in the same state. My mother's definition of soon could be as much as four years.

My show resumed where I left off, on a hot and heavy lesbian sex scene. "I'm going out on a date with a woman," I replied. "Two of them actually. Sorry, Mom, gotta go. Long day at the spa and all."

"What?"

"Love is love, right? Talk to you soon, bye!" I hung up, silenced the ringer, and tossed the phone aside.

I will not look. Not gonna break, I told myself, refusing to give my cell a second glance. Mom meant well, but I wanted to find a man on my terms. My budding business was everything to me, and I wasn't going to let some guy disrupt my focus.

So what if I was the aquatics version of a crazy cat lady?

3

TAYLOR

"*A*re you ready to do this?" Nadir asked.

I glanced at my squad mate and long-time pal. He wore his hair long and loose against his shoulders like an Arab Fabio. He'd infiltrated so many terrorist cells the marines had granted him a permanent pass to break grooming standards.

"I don't have much of a choice," I replied. "Ian is counting on this."

"That's true," he agreed.

"What I don't understand is why the local police department can't handle the matter now that their crooked chief is gone."

"Because," Nadir said, "there are only five or six men on staff. It takes months of dedicated investigation following, observing, and stalking targets to put together a good case. Because the local police department doesn't have the authority we've been granted. We can play hard with the rules."

"But why not tell the new chief?"

"Plausible deniability. Ian believes the new man is as honest as they come, but we don't want to put him in an awkward situation."

"You don't trust his acting to be up to par, eh?"

"That too," Nadir said, grinning. "With the governor coming up for re-election soon, we have his power behind us. He wants this sewn up before elections next year so he can take credit for the decline in drug-related violence."

"Which means we better not fuck this up by leaking information to the wrong people. I don't know what he's scared about. He only has one true opponent and the guy gives me the creeps whenever I see him on the news."

"Yeah, but he's rich, and wealth is power in this state," Nadir said. "So have you rehearsed your story?"

"Hell yeah. I figured I'd go meet this guy tomorrow, come clean about my phony record, and say the Deuce sent me."

In the month since the attempted murder on the rec yard, I'd learned the man knew a hit was coming for him. He'd counted on my arrival, and his right-hand man at the prison let me know I'd performed to expectations. I was the kind of guy they were looking for.

"Well, I'm prepared to help you as much as needed since Ian and Russ aren't able."

"Yeah, law-abiding citizens can't be seen in the company of an ex-con. I get it, but don't have to like being isolated in this little shithole."

We passed through the unfamiliar residential area of Quickdraw. The place was new to me despite two of our friends living outside of the city limits. Here, I was a stranger, and the two of us were studied by curious, but friendly, faces peering through the half-lowered windows.

"What kind of place did you rent me?"

"It's not horrible."

I groaned. "If you gotta start it off by saying 'it's not horrible,' man…"

We pulled off the street and into a pebble drive in front of a small house without a garage. The neighbors waved to us, a family of two adults and four kids. I waved back as I stepped from the car and stared at the shack in front of me.

Peeling paint, torn screens, and rotting wood window shutters were part of my new home. I sighed. "It could be worse," I muttered under my breath.

"Here's the keys. You're paid up for six months," Nadir said when we reached the stoop.

We stepped inside and saw the interior matched the outside down to the yellowing water stains on the white ceiling. He must have rented the oldest place on the block. The floors were laminate and clean, but scratched and peeling. I had a master bedroom of less than average size, a smaller bedroom as big as my closet back home, and one bathroom.

There was an old, musty smell in the air, and the lingering scent of cigarette smoke, which had darkened the curtains and stained the walls.

"The guy who owned this place died of lung cancer a couple months back, I guess. His daughter rented it to me for cheap when I said an ex-con friend of mine would need a place to stay."

I grimaced. "Not surprising." I glanced at the forty-two-inch television and PlayStation 3 on a small, modest entertainment stand. "You brought my stuff?"

"Yeah. Your brother and I brought some things from your place a couple days ago."

My first stop was the bathroom for a shower while Nadir amused himself with my PlayStation 3. Once I finished washing away the prison funk, we made plans to fetch my Cadillac from Houston the next day then went to choke down some burgers from the fast food spot down the road.

"Come on. Admit it. This place isn't so bad," Nadir said.

"Yeah, for being out in the middle of nowhere," I replied. "I'll try to view it as a vacation. Hell, at least I can roam and hunt wild game."

Nadir scrutinized his burger. "This tastes like despair and greasy sadness. We should have hunted instead of buying fast food."

"Agreed, bro."

"Anyway, I'll be in town Saturday night," Nadir said. "Mom and Dad colluded with a friend to set me up and I've been invited to dinner."

I smirked, amused by Nadir's disgruntled frown. "Family on the first date, huh? Poor bastard."

"Yeah, laugh it up. Anyway, afterward, I can meet you up in the woods near Ian's for a hunt. That late, maybe we can drag Russ out with us, too."

"Maybe. Don't be so sure on it," I replied. Russell became such a homebody after the birth of his son that the rest of us rarely saw him anymore. Ever since Dani had questioned his desire to be the stay-at-home parent, he'd taken his job above and beyond the call of duty. Shit. Even a kid needed to experience the great outdoors sometime, right? Juni even offered to make a bear-sized baby sling if it would get him outside with all of us again.

"Yeah, I know."

We tossed our trash, drank a couple of beers, and then Nadir was on his way. True to his word, we drove down into Houston the next day, giving me the chance to check out my auto body shop. I'd trusted my baby to my little brother and right-hand man, Oscar. He thought my undercover jail time was karma for all the years I'd picked on him.

Later, after driving back in my newly detailed Caddie, I secured a job at Tito's Scrapyard & Auto. In my first hour on shift, I learned the place was crooked as a barrel of snakes and one of the other mechanics dealt pot on the side.

This is going to be easy. They don't even try to hide the shit they're doing.

I was on my way back into town from a visit with my brother two days later when I saw her alongside the road. A young woman stood in front of a raised car hood while smoke billowed into the wind. In only a few seconds, I drew conclusions and determined she'd be stuck out in the sun until someone arrived to help.

Not my business. It's not my business.

Through the driver's side window, I caught a glimpse of her brown sugar skin, neatly pinned black hair, and the sharp, curve-hugging business suit accenting her body's best features. The sleek pencil skirt made her look like some kind of fertility goddess, drawing my attention right to her hips.

She was on her way somewhere important. Had to be.

Fuck. Why can't I ever mind my own business? I wondered. A second later, I'd pulled into a gas station half a mile down the interstate then rounded back to park behind her. As I left my car and shut the door behind me, she moved back a step to remain on guard.

"Can I do something to…?" The offer died on my lips as the wind kicked up, kissing my acute sense of smell with cinnamon, cardamom, and some other unique scent. Spicy and sweet, like the foxy woman in front of me. I stared.

"Can you what?" she asked, defensive and wary.

"I… help? With your car?" I finally asked. The world around me—open interstate, speeding cars, and rumbling Mack trucks—became insignificant, and the only thing I could see was her gorgeous face. All that mattered was her big brown eyes and glossy, pouting lips.

Mine. She was meant to be mine. And I'd do anything I had to for her to realize we were fated for each other. Swallowing down the nervous tension clenching my throat, I put on an easygoing smile.

"All of a sudden, my car got really hot, and I have no idea what the hell happened."

"Mind if I take a look?" She waved me toward the engine, but kept her eyes on me like I was some stalker preparing to shove her into my car.

Smart girl. Fuck. Why now of all times? Stumbling across the woman I was meant to love while I was pretending to be a drug-dealing loser was the last thing I expected or wanted.

I waved off the steam pouring from the radiator and engine.

"Your radiator is busted, ma'am."

She cussed under her breath and looked at the time on her cell phone. "Figures, on the day I need it the most…"

"You headed somewhere important?"

"Yeah. I'm signing for a business loan today, and I need to get all the way to Houston to my bank. If I don't do it today, it'll have to wait until after the weekend…"

"And you were all excited about doing it now, am I right?"

She nodded.

"I'll give you a ride," I offered. "Are you from around here?"

"Yeah, I live in Quickdraw. I know I can get a ride home from my friend who works there, but I can't just leave my car alongside the road like this all day. Ugh. Maybe if…" Her finger slid down the phone screen, probably scrolling through contacts in her list. "I can ask my dad if one of his friends can tow it to Tito's."

"So after I drop you off, I'll come back for your ride and drop it off at Tito's."

One of her perfectly shaped brows arched. "And I'm supposed to trust you with my car keys while I'm fifty miles away?"

"You're in big luck 'cause I happen to *work* at Tito's now." I grinned, amused by her wide-eyed expression. "I'm normally under hoods, but I have experience with a tow truck. Go ahead. Verify it."

After she scrutinized my driver's license and phoned the boss, she returned it to me with a faint smile.

"Okay, Taylor. I'll accept your offer. I'm Jada."

"Nice to meet you, ma'am. I—" She raised her phone to snap a picture of me.

"What the hell?"

Jada maneuvered around in to the back of my Cadillac and snapped another photo of the license plate.

"What are you doing?"

"In case I go missing," she replied.

I stared at her.

"You can never be too safe," Jada insisted. "Besides, my dad wouldn't ever let me hear the end of it if he knew I was hitchhiking with a stranger."

"Yeah? Who's your dad?" After she slipped into the passenger seat, I shut the door and crossed to my side.

"Chief Hunt."

I cut my eyes over to the sexy girl in my passenger seat. Jada's exotic features and ochre skin tone clashed with my memories of a sandy-haired white guy at the Quickdraw police station. "Huh?"

"He's my stepdad," Jada explained. "He adopted me when he married my mom, but... well, he's just Dad to me. I love him. He's the only father I've ever known." Her eyes twinkled as if she had more to say on the subject, but she bit her tongue.

"That's cool." I took my eyes off her curves and focused on the road. "So which bank we heading to?"

"Prime Advantage Bank of Texas. It's at... ugh, wait. I'll just add it to my GPS."

"No, it's cool. I know the way there. I use that bank. Great coincidence, huh?"

I should have figured as much, and I was happy I'd only be dropping her off. As much as I'd love to see Daniela, we had to pretend to be strangers.

"So, you said a business loan," I prompted. A steady current from the air conditioner stirred her scent, subjecting me to the worst torture I'd ever experienced. It took all of my willpower to focus on the road instead of my increasing desire to get my head between her thighs.

"I'm expanding my business," she replied without giving any detail.

Wary girl. Guess that's a good thing. I'd dated a few girls who gave me their whole life story on the first meeting, which left no mystery to unravel later. Boring. "Oh yeah? What do you do?"

"I own the salon and day spa in town."

"Oh, I've passed by there. It's just across the street from the garage. Can't say I have any need to visit a spa, though."

"You'd be surprised," Jada said, opening up a bit more. "We cut men's hair and I have a couple clients who get regular massages." She glanced at me, and for the first time, a smile spread over her face. "One of my friends, her husband comes in for manscaping regularly. He's like a bear."

Fucking Russ. It's gotta be. Choking back my laughter was an exercise in futility, so I let it loose. "I don't even wanna know what all's involved with manscaping. Sounds painful."

"It's not that bad," she insisted. "When I wax guys, I get it done and over with quickly."

I winced. "I don't think you could pay me to lie down for a wax." I wasn't all that hairy anyway, unlike Russ who looked like he was settling down for a winter's hibernation. My body hair was fine and soft, the same tawny brown as my pelt when I took my cougar form. It blended with my skin.

"It's really not as bad as Hollywood makes it out to be." Jada's husky chuckle raised goose bumps on my skin. I imagined the sultry sound huffed against my ear, a bad decision I came to regret when my stiffening dick pressed against my jeans.

I shivered.

"You okay?" she asked, concerned.

"Yeah, I'm fine," I lied. "Anyway, I'll pop in for a trim one day."

Once she succeeded in gaining my agreement to enter her shop, Jada changed topics and told me about some of Quickdraw's popular spots. All two of them.

"So on Thursday and Friday nights, a lot of people go to the VFW Hall for bingo nights. Any other time, there's a little sports bar at the edge of town with cheap beer and overpriced alcohol. I think they water the beer down."

"Damn. What the hell does anybody do for fun?"

"Go to Huntsville," she chirped. "There's a country western club and some university bars people like to visit. Aside from that, we don't have much in the actual town."

"At least there's a liquor store," I grumbled. Drinking a beer after work would probably be the highlight of my day.

"Watch your wallet around there after dark, though. The hookers are pickpockets and a couple folk have been roughed up."

"Y'all's town has hookers? Like actual hos and prostitutes?" Snickering, I merged with the main highway and caught a glimpse of the sign. We had nearly an hour to go.

"Doesn't every place?"

"True enough. So their pimps get physical with folk?"

Jada shrugged. "Rumor says drug exchanges go bad, but the cops never turn up anything."

"Well, thanks for the heads-up."

We chatted the rest of the way, some of it small talk, some of it deeper, meaningful, and hard-earned information she appeared reluctant to give. By the time I dropped her off, I knew all about her struggle to bring better local businesses to her little town, and her dreams for expanding the salon's services.

Before she left my car, I got her to accept my phone number and input hers into my phone.

The timing was crap, but hell if I was going to let her slip through my fingers.

"Thanks, Taylor."

I idled until she was safely through the bank doors before I pulled out from the parking lot. I activated the Bluetooth and impatiently waited until Russ greeted me with a sleep-deprived voice.

"Russ, you won't believe what just happened, man."

"Damnit, Taylor, Mateo is napping and it's my only chance to get some shut-eye myself."

"Screw sleep, this is more important."

"I'm gonna beat your a—"

"I found her."

"You found who, you flea-ridden fuzzball?" Russell grouched.

"*Her,*" I breathed, still shocked by the discovery. "You and Ian are starting a damn trend."

The gruffness in Russell's voice faded in an instant. "Holy crap, for real? Who is she, man?"

"Your manscaper." I had to get a small dig in while I could.

"Who? My man—no way! You mean Jada?"

"She's the one, Russ. And ha! You admit to getting waxed."

"Look, y'all know my back is awful. I look like I'm trapped between a shift or something. So one day, Dani sort of offhandedly mentioned... we're not about to have this damned conversation right now. What happened with Jada?"

I relayed the day's events, starting with spotting her broken down car all the way up to dropping her off.

"How did you stand it?" I asked him.

"Resisting?" Russ guessed, too insightful for his own good.

"I wanted to pull over to rip her clothes off." Our animal halves could be exceptionally focused, single-minded creatures. Ian had admitted his eagle had two modes, consisting of sating his hunger for food or his new wife. I'd envied him until now.

"It didn't kick in for me right off, remember? I was still mourning Katie." Russ quieted for a moment. He never really did stop grieving, and that was fine, the mating bond was a powerful thing to deny even in death. "When I finally realized Dani was the one for me, hell, I was already about to bond with her. So I guess I never did resist it."

"I better call Ian next, huh?"

"You better. With you being undercover, it's going to be hard pulling off a love affair."

"The timing is shit. What do I do, though? Ignore her and make a move later? What if she moves on?"

"Hey, don't forget, man, if she's really *the* one, she'll be drawn to you, too."

His words should have reassured me, but I had a feeling this whole thing was going to be a tricky balancing act. Good things cats always landed on their feet.

4

JADA

*D*aniela and I stopped at IHOP to celebrate the approval of my business loan. I was floating on cloud nine, so happy I could barely sit still while we perused the menus.

"Thanks for giving me the ride. Let me cover the bill, okay?"

"It's no big deal, sheesh. You don't even charge me a fraction of what you should for my hair."

"I know what they charge in Houston, but that's not why I opened a business. Most of the people in Quickdraw are older with retirement pensions and limited income, you know? Why would I want to charge Granny a hundred bucks for a deep condition, trim, and roller set?"

"True. So, what about that guy who dropped you

off? I had to look at his photo twice after you sent it. He's sexy as hell."

"I know! His eyes are unreal." I slid my phone from the table for another glance at Taylor's handsome face. He had chiseled good looks, like a male fashion model caught off the runway. I imagined the body beneath his tee and oil-stained jeans, picturing a flawless physique of lean muscle and tight abs. "And he's sweet, too. I know that shouldn't be an afterthought, but most guys like him act like I should feel lucky they want to be with me."

"And this one?"

"We just laughed and talked most of the way once he broke the ice. I kept trying to shut him down, but he didn't give up. He's amazing."

"Well?" Daniela gave me a look.

"Well what?"

"You're single, and he's new to town…"

"How do you know he's new to town?"

Daniela pursed her lips and shot me a mischievous look. "Well, I kinda saw him yesterday when I took my car in for an oil change. I don't let Russ touch my baby. He's great when it comes to guns and all of that stuff, but he doesn't know the first thing about upkeep for a vehicle."

"Ahh, gotcha. So he worked on your car."

She nodded. "Friendly guy. New to town," she repeated.

"Probably not single," I interjected.

"Didn't he give you his number?"

I rolled my eyes and turned to face the approaching waitress. We placed our orders before continuing the conversation. "Yeah, but I'm pretty sure it wasn't for personal calls. He has my car keys, remember?"

"Oh." Dani looked disappointed.

My friend brought Taylor up again on the way home, asking if I planned to give him a call about more than the car.

"Oh goodness, no. I told you, I'm probably not his type. Those kinds of guys always want a girl like the chick in the workout videos I loaned you. Look at me. He'd get lost in my fat." I groaned into one hand. I carried a lot of weight in my breasts and ass, but especially in the hips where golden stretch marks streaked my skin. Guys loved my hourglass figure until the clothes came off and they saw my volup- tuous silhouette included tiger stripes, too.

"What rolls?" Dani asked irritably. "You're smaller than I am."

"You just had a baby."

"I'm only five pounds heavier than I was before I had Mateo. I've been this size for years, and I'm okay with it now. Wouldn't you say Russ is one of *those kinds of guys?*"

I shot her a skeptical look. "Just because some fairy godmother blessed you and Leigh with sexy-as-fuck men, doesn't mean she's got a third one hidden for me."

"And how will you know without checking it out?" Dani demanded.

"I don't know. Maybe. I'm just trying to focus on work, you know?"

Daniela reached across the center console and took my hand. "Live a little, huh? The loan is secured, meaning the shop space next door will officially be yours and your spa is going to be a hit. I think you deserve a good guy in that mix, too."

"Dani—"

"Or at least a good lay. When was the last time you got some, chica?"

My cheeks never showed a blush well, but I always felt the heat creeping into my face. "A couple years," I muttered. "It's definitely, ah, been a while."

A vision flitted through my mind of returning to Tito's and finding Taylor under the hood, his coveralls tied around his waist to reveal a sculpted upper body. He'd be all muscles and lean angles, like a statue carved from sandstone. A golden brown Adonis with beautiful topaz-blue eyes. I must have stared into them at least a dozen times on the way.

"Okay. You win, you win. I'll call him tonight."

~

"*H*ow did everything go?"

"From crappy to good," I answered my mother while I washed my hands in the sink.

"What happened?"

"My car broke down on the way to the bank."

"If your car's in the shop, how'd get you get to Houston?" Danny asked. He noisily chewed a handful of Oreos while loitering in front of the pantry. I shot my little brother a dirty look. In a few months, he and his buddies would be heading off to boot camp, so he was enjoying one last summer with us at home.

"You'll ruin your dinner, Daniel. Put them away." My mom shook a finger at him. "Now, what was it you were saying, Jada?"

I bit my lip and turned to start dicing the vegetables for the night's salad. "Daniela Reyes gave me a ride home."

"Nice girl. Speaking of which, the wedding invitations arrived today. Not for another three months, but I guess with so much family out of the state and country they wanted to get them out early. Did you know Russell's mother lives in Russia?"

I shook my head. Insignificant facts easily amused my mother, but the news didn't surprise me; the guy was built like a Russian wrestler. "I wonder if that's why he's named Russ," I mused.

"You said ride home, though. How'd you *get* there," Danny asked. Ignoring Mom, he popped another Oreo into his mouth. I figured some of it stemmed from a desire to binge on things while he could. There wouldn't be cookies in basic training.

The front door opened and shut. After a thrilling day of keeping the peace in Quickdraw, my dad usually thundered into the house, showered, then collapsed somewhere to play a boring tactical warfare game on his laptop. He poked his head into the kitchen first and brightened when he saw me.

"Hi, guys. Joining us for dinner tonight, too, baby?"

"Hi, Daddy. I—"

"Jada hitched a ride into the city," Danny snitched promptly.

"You little asshole," I shot at my grinning brother, hurling a pot holder at him.

"You took a ride from who?" Dad asked. He twisted to stare at me.

Kid brothers. Ugh. "His name's Taylor Jackson.

He's really sweet and gave me a ride to Houston, and then he wouldn't even accept gas money from me for the trouble."

"Taylor Jackson," he repeated in a low voice. I recognized the look on my father's face, his expression darkening like storm clouds. He was trying to place the name with known troublemakers in the area. "Doesn't ring a bell."

I sighed in relief. "He works at the garage and is fairly new to town, so lay off a little, okay?"

Dad grunted and let it slide. Once he left the kitchen, I approached Danny to recover the pot holder. I stole a few of his cookies, too.

"Shouldn't you watch what you eat, Jada?"

Mom's words cut through me, a cold knife trimming the elation from my chipper mood. I sighed and started to put them back, but Danny pushed my hand away and shook his head.

"Eat them," he mouthed at me.

I tried, but the taste and desire for sweets was ruined by my mother's perpetual need to point out my weight at every opportunity.

During dinner, Mom didn't miss a chance to quiz me about Taylor.

Probably worried I won't show any interest in her military playboy from Houston if I find someone on my own, I thought bitterly. She'd probably promised my cooperation to the guy's dad like we were back to the days of dowries and courting. Doctor Hazim Zaman was a nice guy, or so I thought the single time I met him, but too old fashioned for my tastes.

I escaped the house as soon as I could, but the phone rang as soon as I stepped through my front door. My parents must have some kind of x-ray sense, a vision allowing them to see clear across town into my living room. That or they called my neighbors and asked if my car was in the drive yet. Both options rated high on the Creep-o-Meter.

A glance at the caller ID revealing Dad's number. I sighed. "Hi, Daddy."

"Did he tell you he's fresh out of lockup?" Dad asked.

"Huh?"

"Your new friend. Did he tell you he's been in prison? He has a list of—"

"You looked him up?" My voice raised, sharpening more on each word. My dad had always been tough on any guy I dated, but he'd never run one of my boyfriends through the system before. Worse, I hadn't even been asked on a date with Taylor yet.

"I sure did," he growled. "The name sounded familiar, so I asked Marty about him. The kid has a criminal record rivaling an east coast rapper. It's a wonder he isn't still behind bars."

"Daddy, did you seriously have Marty run a background check on Taylor the moment I left the house?"

"I did, and I don't regret it either." He sighed. "Jada, you deserve better than a thug. Why don't you take a lesson from your friend Leigh Denton and stay clear of troublemakers, okay?"

Before Leigh married Ian MacArthur, she'd gotten knocked up by one of the local pot dealers. My dad locked him up for selling stolen narcotics before she even had their baby.

I'd felt so bad for her then. Now she had a happy marriage and a bright future for her daughter.

"Okay, Daddy. He did a nice thing for me, but I didn't plan to hang around him, if that's what you're worried about. I'm gonna go to bed now though, okay?"

"I didn't mean to upset you, punkin."

"I'm not upset," I assured him. Miffed, exhausted, wishing sometimes I could make my own life's choices, but not upset. "I'm really tired, and I have a lot of stuff to do tomorrow with the spa."

"Okay. I love you."

"Love you, too."

I tossed the phone onto my bed on my way to the restroom where I drew a hot bath. I poured a generous amount of orange blossom bath salts into the steaming water then soaked while an audiobook played from my Kindle.

With business on the rise and an expansion in the works for my day spa, I didn't need to invite trouble into my life. I lay down in bed an hour later, forcing the memory of Taylor's smile from my thoughts.

I knew it was too good to be true.

At least I had a planned shopping trip with the girls.

*J*ada didn't call. I'd expected as much to happen once gossip spread about my so-called past. Daniela and Leigh both called to chat about her, but Jada's number never showed up on my call list, despite their efforts to convince her to give me a chance.

Nadir had the same shitty luck. His blind date for the weekend bailed. Her parents apologized profusely, fed him well, and then he showed up at my place for a few rounds of video games on my PlayStation over beers. Neither of us wanted to hunt in our crappy moods. We'd slaughter half the forest.

"Were you actually looking forward to meeting your mystery chick?"

"Yeah, maybe," he grumbled. "Would be nice to

have what you three found, you know?" My pal hesitated for a moment then asked, "Have you seen Sasha recently?"

I shook my head.

"She's pretty depressed."

I sighed. "I know. I really wanted to be that man for them, too. Honest, dude. Her sisters are amazing women, but there just wasn't anything there beyond the sex and our friendship. You know what happened. If I stayed with them, we would have gone through that again."

"I know," Nadir said sadly. "I'm sorry for that. I only meant to say that you should call her. She blames herself even after all this time."

My ex-girlfriend Sasha was in a soul-mated partnership with two other lionesses. They'd wanted me to be their alpha, their pride's male, and I'd given it my all until the inevitable happened.

I still emailed Nandi, the youngest lioness of their pride. As much as I adored them, I couldn't give them what they truly needed.

At least I'd found my mate, even if she didn't know it. Nadir had no one.

Screw it. If she's not going to come to me, I'll go to her. If she's not interested, then I need to hear it from her mouth.

I made a visit to her salon on my first day off,

hopeful Ian's plan hadn't blown my chance with my one and only. If I was lucky, there was a logical reason behind the extended silence... like dropping her phone in the sink or letting the days slip away from her with work.

Probably not. I had a feeling Ian's top secret plan had fucked me good.

A sign above the doors read *Nirvana* in cursive, golden font. Smaller, plain white letters beneath the store name indicated, 'salon and spa services'. The place was tucked between a vacant building and a thrift store.

I opened the door and stepped inside, finding myself treated to gentle music suited for meditation and the spicy scent of sandalwood, vanilla, and jasmine. A sexy brunette approached from behind the counter, clothed in a tiny strapless dress. Her blue eyes dragged over me from head to toe. "Can I help you, sir?" she drawled.

Glancing over the main room revealed no sign of Jada until I noticed her unattended purse at a nearby station. "Actually... yeah. Y'all got a barber here?" I asked.

"That's me. I'm Lisa. Whatcha need done?"

"Fade me up." I'd pay for a haircut if it could stall until Jada appeared to see me.

I settled in the chair and offered my name to the

spiky haired girl as she fastened the black drape around me.

"Hope you don't mind me saying this, but your eyes are gorgeous, Taylor."

I chuckled. "Thanks. I get that a lot."

"So, are you new in town?"

"Yeah. Rented a place over on Davenport Street. I work for Big Tito."

Lisa's trimmers began their work as she engaged me in casual chitchat. I watched her in the mirror.

Too skinny, I thought. I'd always liked plump girls with hips. Something I could squeeze and hold onto during sex. A girl I could fuck hard without fearing I'd break her. A girl who could carry her weight with confidence without giving a damn about what anyone thought but me and her. Lisa was pretty, but the attraction was nonexistent.

Jada had me firmly under her spell, fantasizing about how soft she'd feel in my arms, the sweet scent of her skin, and how much I wanted to taste her lips on mine.

"How's that look?" Lisa asked, interrupting my fantasies about Jada.

Taking some time to admire my reflection in the mirror first, I couldn't find a thing to complain about.

"Looks great. Thanks. What do I owe you?"

"Fifteen."

I gave her a twenty instead and told her to keep the change.

"Here's my card and my number, you know... in case you wanna be a repeat customer sometime. You can gimme a call whenever or—" her brown eyes drifted down to my pocket and the cell phone inside it "—you can text me at that number. Any time."

"Hey, Lisa, I'm gonna go—"

I twisted toward the source of the voice to find Jada framed in the doorway at the salon's rear, staring at me.

"Hi, Jada."

"Hi," she replied, guarded.

"You two know each other?" The disappointment blossomed on Lisa's face, her expression falling like toast, jelly side down.

"I gave her a ride to Houston the other day," I offered, remaining vague. I stepped from beside Lisa and approached Jada at the back of the room.

"Got some time to talk?"

"What do you want to talk about?" she asked.

"Why you didn't call. Did I do something? Did I upset you?"

"You didn't upset me." She fidgeted.

"Then what's wrong? We were all cool when you got out of the car, now you can barely look at me."

"You didn't tell me you were fresh out of prison."

I sighed. A quick glance to Lisa's direction revealed her sweeping the mess by her station while pretending not to eavesdrop. Her eyes had grown wide.

"So I did some time."

"You didn't tell me that."

"It's not exactly the first thing I cough up when I meet someone. How'd you find out?" I asked, trying to play it safe.

"My dad told me. Word gets around in a small town, so I guess one of your homies down at Tito's must have spread the word."

Damnit. I knew this was going to happen. "Please, hear me out."

She hesitated, brown eyes fixed to my face. "Why were you in jail?"

"I didn't kill anyone, Jada. I'm not a rapist, child molester, or a murderer. I made some mistakes that put me in a bad situation. That's all. I served my time." I hadn't lied to her yet; I made the mistake of letting Ian talk me into this mess, and I'd never laid an aggressive hand on a woman in all of my life. Kids were great, and I'd sooner fuck someone up for harming a child.

"What. Did. You. Do?" Jada repeated, enunciating the words.

With a heavy heart, I told her the crimes in my file. She'd probably look me up by name later to see the phony record in the system, if she didn't have her dad do it.

"My conviction is for assault and battery. I have a couple small possession charges, too."

"Are you a dopehead?"

"I don't do drugs."

"So you deal them." Disgust laced her voice. "Get out."

So much for Russell's claim about fated mates feeling mutual attraction. I didn't have a chance, and I wouldn't hang around to beg like the damned dog shifter at Big Tito's.

I held on to my dignity and walked out.

～

JADA

*L*isa stared at me when the door shut. "I can't believe you let that sexy-ass man walk out of here because he *used* to deal drugs."

"It's a pretty damning background."

She shrugged. "Everybody makes mistakes."

"You know as well as I do that shady business

happens across the street. It's like he got out of prison and went right back to it."

Lisa shrugged a second time. "Ain't got anything to do with me. Or you. So he got a job — a good paying job, I might add — at a shop that's got a reputation. Doesn't mean he's dealing. It's better than no job, right?"

"I guess."

"He gave you a ride to Houston, girl, without wanting anything in return. Didn't he have Tito cut you a deal on that new radiator, too? Shit, when mine had that leak, he charged me about eight hundred dollars."

"So? Giving me a ride and a discount on some work doesn't mean he's a law-abiding citizen now."

"I'm just saying give him a chance and find out instead of assuming." Lisa glanced toward the door. "If you don't want him, can I have him?"

"What kind of question is that?" I demanded.

"Well, if I walk over there and chat him up again, are you going to flip tables later over it?"

"I kinda sent him packing, so why should I care?"

"Because I know you. You'll regret it later and wonder if you made a bad mistake. You'll feel *awful*."

Sulking, I glanced at my phone. "I'll give him one date." *Daddy is gonna hate it. Good thing I'm a grown woman now. Lisa's right. I'd feel terrible. Hell, I already feel terrible for how I treated him just now.*

Taylor answered on the first ring, a little overenthusiastic for my tastes, but a pleasant change from the usual guys who played games. "Hello, Ms. Hunt." He sounded like a kicked puppy, contradicting my previous idea regarding his enthusiasm. The guilt washed over me anew.

"Dinner, Lottie's Italian Cafe, seven o'clock."

"Huh?"

"You want a chance, I'm giving you one. So don't be late."

Lisa flashed me a thumb's up. After I ended the call, she forced me into my own salon chair and plucked the curling irons out of the cradle.

"You can't go on a date looking like this."

"What? I'm not trying to impress him." *Not yet.*

"He just got out of prison. He probably hasn't been laid in *years.*"

"I'm not planning to have sex with him on the first date!" I cried.

"I'm just sayin'. Take some protection with you anyway, girl."

I rolled my eyes. My hair was so sleek and straight it was impossible for me to get a curl into it. Lisa had a secret with the hair spray and a method for pinning them afterward. By the time they fell for my date, I'd have lovely, loose, mermaid waves.

"Don't you dare show up without dressing sexy," Lisa warned me as I headed out the door half an hour later.

"It's only a first date."

"With a man who looks like he belongs on GQ's cover," she shot back at me.

"His looks aren't why I like him."

"Ha! I knew you liked him!"

Once home from the salon, I pulled out a black dress with a fitted waist and sweetheart neckline. Ever since high school, I'd had trouble squeezing into dresses without stretchy busts and flowy skirts. The hem fluttered two inches above my knees, modest but sexy without danger of showing him my panties. Paired with strappy wedges, I looked and felt amazing.

Lottie's Italian Cafe was one of the nicer eateries in town. Nice as in there was an actual wine menu. I arrived on foot at a quarter to seven, expecting to wait for Taylor, but I entered to find him already at a table. He'd traded in his worn jeans and t-shirt for khaki slacks and a button-down shirt.

Damn, he cleans up nice.

Taylor stood and seated me like a gentleman. "I

ordered some wine. I hope you don't mind. An old friend recommended one."

"A friend from prison or before that?"

"Before that." He had a warm, endearing laugh paired with a smile capable of melting ice. "My friend Nadir is practically a career wine snob. If it comes in a bottle, he's had it, no matter what part of the world it comes from."

"Nadir?" Both of my brows shot up. "My folks had a Nadir over for dinner this past weekend." *What are the odds?*

"A marine named Nadir?" Taylor asked.

"With a year left before discharge," I replied.

"Small world. I didn't realize your families were close," Taylor said. He took a long gulp from his ice water.

"His dad and my mom both work at the same hospital in The Woodlands. I was, uh, kinda supposed to be there. For a date." I cleared my throat and took a sip of wine to wash the sour taste from my mouth.

"So you're the one who stood him up?"

"I had good reason! My mom told me about it after I promised my friends Dani and Leigh I'd go south of Houston with them," I defended myself. My ears burned.

"Chill, it's cool. I mean, it's not like he cried or

anything. He was kinda bummed he came all this way out to Quickdraw, but then we zoned in front of the PlayStation a few hours and all was good."

Desperate to ease the growing tension between us, without even understanding why it mattered, I gripped onto a possible change of topic. "Got a PS3 or PS4?"

"The three. I've bought way too much to upgrade systems now," he replied.

So he's a former drug dealer who likes to video game when he isn't peddling weed, I thought. With the menu spread open before me, I perused the entrees and made a quick selection before the waitress returned to take our orders.

"So... am I right if I assume you're a gamer, too? What's your favorite game?" he asked.

Leaning forward, I watched him from across the table. His bright blue eyes held mine, shameless and inquisitive. For the first time, there was a man interested in what *I* liked to do.

"I'm hopelessly addicted to Minecraft," I admitted. "I built a full out city with a mine down to the lava pits and everything."

"Nadir and I build sky cities in creative mode when we're not playing Borderlands," he confessed. "Creepers piss me off too much to deal with them."

"I have that game, but I kinda suck at it." I shrugged. "Maybe we can play sometime though."

It seemed a perfectly reasonable and innocent suggestion. We were both saved from an immediate reply by the arrival of our food. Afraid of looking like a pig in front of my hunky date, I ordered a light mushroom ravioli and soup instead of my preferred meal.

Taylor had a sixth sense. He saw through the bullshit and eyed my plate like it was an alien creature. "That's it? That's all you're gonna eat?"

"Ravioli is filling."

"For about five minutes maybe," he retorted. "That's a *snack*, not a dinner. Here, try the shrimp."

He passed over two large shellfish from his plate without making a dent. Wafts of lemon and garlic-scented steam made my mouth water with anticipation.

Damn him. I love shrimp.

By the time we cleared our plates, he'd snuck several more shrimp over for me to eat.

"No dessert?"

"I'm watching my weight," I replied uneasily.

Taylor's brows rose. "Okay…"

Ugh. Leave it to a guy to make me feel awkward about it. "I'm always nibbling on sweets, so I try not to overdo it."

"You know, you're sexy as hell the way you look now."

The compliment brought a rush of pleasure. "Yeah, well, you're not so bad looking yourself."

Who was I kidding?

He was absolutely fucking gorgeous, and as far as I could see, his personality matched.

~

"*I* saved you! Ha! Ha!" I threw up both of my arms and whooped in victory, rubbing it in until Taylor shot me a look from his side of the couch.

"I softened him up for you," he grumbled in his sexy baritone. He sulked the way my brother would when I beat him at a fighting game.

"You were hiding around the corner almost dead," I shot back.

Maybe first-person shooter games weren't so bad after all, or maybe it was the company and his easy-going smiles.

I don't know what happened. One moment, he was sharing his cannoli with me — since I refused to order dessert — in the next, I was accepting a last-minute invitation to game with him for a couple hours after dinner.

"I won fair and square. Now pay up." I grinned and shifted on the couch, stretching out my legs toward him.

I'd never received a foot rub from a man before, especially not on the first date. His electrifying touch sent sparks up my calves and warmed my skin. Thank God I'd recently waxed. His fingers were magic, introducing me to a slice of the heaven I gift to my clients at the shop.

"You've done this before," I accused.

"Not as many times as you're probably thinking," he replied.

I didn't have anything to say on it because I didn't want to begin to imagine his hands on some other woman's feet. Or anywhere on her, really. So I closed my eyes and enjoyed the relaxing massage.

"Hey," I asked, "what time is it anyway?"

"Going on ten."

Ten o'clock already? Crap. I opened my eyes and reluctantly slid my feet from his lap. His hands were like magic.

"I should probably head home. Time ran away."

"Always does when you're having fun. I'm glad we did this, Jada."

"Me too."

He walked me to the door and opened it for me. I

stepped out, but paused in the doorway to turn around and look back at him.

"Thanks for um… a fun time," I said. The man in front of me contradicted everything about the record my dad shared with me over the phone. He was sweet, respectful, and I didn't catch even a whiff of drugs in his place. His bathroom was clean and tidy, and the rest of the home was small, but undecorated.

New. A fresh start.

Taylor had served his time, and I wouldn't be the asshole to deny him a second chance. Surrendering to my impulses, I stepped in and grabbed him by the shirt collar for a kiss, my heels bringing me to the perfect height for our lips to meet.

If his massages were bliss, his kisses were sin incarnate. Carnal desire jolted straight through me, dampening my panties and making my pussy clench. His tongue didn't meekly explore my mouth, it laid claim, and I mirrored his hungry enthusiasm.

"Wow," he murmured against my lips.

Wow indeed. He kissed me again, equally unwilling to part. His strong arms enfolded me, tugging me in close to his hard body.

No. I am not gonna fuck him on our first date, I chided myself. I wanted to, though. I had the craziest urge to push back through the doorway and rip all his clothes off. I felt him hardening against me and imagined the thick cock waiting beneath a layer of khaki. My fingers burned to slip between our bodies for a touch.

Stepping backward, I distanced myself until I moved down from the steps. "I'll see you this weekend?"

"Yeah... this weekend's great."

"Or earlier if you want." I bit my lower lip and watched for his reaction. His blue eyes lit up.

"I'm free after work tomorrow, too."

"Good. I'll see you then."

"Sure you don't want a ride?" he asked, dubious. "It's dark out. Why don't you let me drive you instead?"

I chuckled and shook my head. "No, a little walk won't hurt me." I smiled one last time and hurried out onto the road. Most neighborhoods in Quick-draw lacked sidewalks, forcing residents to follow the side of the road. I lived two streets over from Taylor, farther away from the business quarter.

Long stretches of darkness spanned between Main Street's occasional streetlamp. Outside of the downtown business strip, the residential communities sat in relative darkness, lit by only their own garden lamps and porch lights.

The cool night breeze ruffled through my hair,

carrying the faint stench from a pair of nearby dumpsters. After raising my purse higher up my shoulder, I hurried across the narrow street. Taylor lived on my side of town, thankfully, half a mile from the police station and down the road from my shop.

I traveled a road lined by quiet homes, my placid neighborhood tucked behind the town's only veterinary clinic. A dog barked to my right, my neighbor's black and white border collie greeting me. Across the road, two teens smoked on the curb, oblivious to my passage.

Certain someone was following me, I clutched my house keys in one hand and my cell phone in the other, prepared to speed dial my dad. Twice, I looked back over my shoulder, but I saw nothing and hurried forward across my driveway.

The headlights of a passing truck illuminated the road, sending shadows over my lawn. They also reflected off a pair of unnaturally bright blue eyes. They shone back at me from the bushes, set in a tawny, feline face.

"Holy shit."

As my heart slammed against my ribs, I fumbled the keys and stepped back onto the porch. The creature didn't move, a silent observer from the bushes. Somehow, I managed to turn the key in the lock and hurry inside, where I immediately went to the window overlooking the yard. A large mountain lion stepped out from between my two hydrangea bushes. It watched me through the window then fell back into the growth.

"What the hell is it doing in town?" I breathed out a relieved sigh and considered calling Animal Control. A wild cougar could cause all sorts of havoc.

I called my father instead.

"Hey, Daddy?"

"What's wrong, punkin?"

"If a big animal like a wolf… or a mountain lion came in town, what would happen?"

"Probably shoot it, darlin'. Why?"

I hesitated. "Is that necessary?"

"Wild animals like that only venture into town when they're hungry, punkin. *Real* hungry. Which makes 'em dangerous. Did you see something tonight?"

Lying to Dad made me feel awful, so I opted for the truth. "I think I saw a mountain lion in my yard. I mean, it's real dark, so maybe I was mistaken."

"I'll send an officer around just to be safe. I'll feel better if you stay in the house tonight."

I shivered and moved to the window again. My

sandy-furred friend hadn't returned. "I don't think he wanted to eat me."

"Like I said, Jada, a wild animal like that doesn't come into town unless it's hungry."

"He could have caught me at any time, Daddy. I mean, he walked right past a couple teenagers across the street and they're still out there smoking."

"You sure you weren't seeing a cat? Mr. Kendall has one of them fancy special breeds and it wouldn't be the first time he's gotten out."

"If it was a house cat, it was on 'roids, 'cause he definitely didn't miss out on leg day. He must hit the gym more than Danny 'cause I've never seen a house cat that tall and buff in all my life."

"Well, I'm glad you called. Lock your door and make sure you turn your porch light on."

"Lock my door? Is the cougar going to pop in for a visit?" I teased.

"Ha ha," he quipped. "Humor me, okay? You should be locking your door anyway, a young woman living alone. You should have a dog over there with you. And a gun."

"What's a dog going to do? Maybe I'll walk outside and recruit my feline stalker," I teased him.

We said our goodbyes, and then I ended the call. By the time I laid my head on my pillow, I was exhausted. Stretching my body along the cool sheets,

I snuggled into the silk and closed my eyes, letting the pillow top mattress embrace my curves.

Sleep came easily, my dreams visited by prowling mountain lions with piercing blue eyes. I couldn't get the animal out of my head.

When Dani and I met for lunch the next day, I told her about the mountain lion and my increasing certainty that I didn't have a close brush with death.

"I felt the same way when I found a black bear in my backyard," Dani said.

"A black bear? Did Russ shoot it?"

"No. This was before Russ and I moved in with each other. Before we were really dating. I came down one morning and this bear was laying in my new hammock."

"Seriously? What did you do about it?" I asked.

"I fed him," Dani answered, laughing. "My dad hated that I did it, but he was miles and miles away, so what was he going to do? Ground me?"

We shared a laugh. The idea of a bear snoozing in her outdoor furniture made me think of Tumblr and America's Funniest Home Videos. "God, I hope you took photos, 'cause I'd love to see that. What happened to him?"

Her eyes twinkled. "Oh, I still see him sometimes. I did take a few photos on my phone of him. I like to imagine he lives on our property because he knows it's safe and I'll always give him food."

I plucked a cheesy, beef-covered nacho from the pile of Tex-Mex on my plate. "Too bad I can't do the same for a mountain lion. Daddy said they're likely to kill him if he's found."

"Better to set food out for a hungry animal than risk it eating a neighbor's house cat or dog, right?"

I crumpled a napkin and tossed it at Dani. "You're such an enabler. Anyway, you live in the boonies. I doubt I'll see Mister Cat again."

"Never say never."

After work, I enjoyed dinner and a movie with Taylor. Despite everything I ever learned about wild animals, I went home and thawed some grilled chicken breast in a dish. My mom, hoping to encourage me to eat smart and lose weight, had brought me a couple pounds of it for salads. I scooped a couple of handfuls into a pie dish and left it outside by the back door.

Then I tried to pretend it wasn't there. By bedtime, I felt silly for wasting good leftovers and was on my way to retrieve it for the trash when I heard a startling noise.

I followed the strange caterwauling sound to my back door and opened it to peer out.

Blue eyes stared up at me from the porch. With a

shriek, I slammed it shut again then scrambled to the window to look outside. The mountain lion lay on his belly beside the empty pan, watching me in return through the window.

Holy shit, Dani was right.

The creature rose to all fours and walked up to my door. He pawed it noisily, scratching the plain wood with his claws.

Did he want more food?

I hid behind the door out of his sight for a few minutes, but when I peeked out the window again, I saw his face right against it, waiting for me. I stumbled back, laughing at the hilarious situation.

"Okay, so you want more food, huh?"

I searched the freezer until I found some ribs I froze after the Labor Day barbecue. After thawing them in the microwave, I slid another dish out the door.

Eventually, after I'd taken a photo and a few videos of him, my majestic friend strolled down the steps and disappeared into the trees beyond my backyard.

I watched him leave and wondered if he'd return again.

"*H*er dad despises me," I grumbled.

Ian chuckled and passed me a beer. "I'm sure that's not true."

"He sent her an assload of texts during our second date before she even got home. Called the whole time we were chillin' at my place. She didn't notice because she'd muted her phone." Jada had called later, warning me her dad might pop around or stop at my job to see me. We nixed our plans for a third night out in favor of waiting a couple days. So I visited her as a cougar again, and found she'd taken Dani's advice to make me a pot roast.

Ian laughed at the story of my visit.

"I'm so glad to amuse you."

"I'm not laughing at you, man. I'm laughing 'cause

you remind me of what I did to Leigh when I showed up at her place. And I'm laughing at Hunt. At this town, I guess. Word spreads fast when you're in a small town. People don't have much to do here besides tell other folks' business.

"Yeah, I know about everything except what we *need* to hear about." Who was dating who was a hot topic and spread like fire. Trying to find out who was dealing to who? Tight lips all around.

"Technically, you shouldn't even be here. You're supposed to use Nadir as your contact to keep us abreast of the situation with Tito and his gang," Ian pointed out.

"Don't be an asshole," I grumbled. "I'm isolated out there and Nadir can't babysit me whenever I get bored."

"You have Jada."

"Jada has a business," I reminded him, "and friends of her own. Besides, it would take another shifter to track down the way I came to get here. I stripped down in the woods at Kayak Pass and ran the rest of the way on foot. Uh, thanks for the clothes by the way, Leigh."

Leigh had tired of housing naked men at all hours of the day. The novelty had worn off after the first month. Now she kept an array of clothes from Goodwill in a basket by the back patio door.

TAYLOR

"You're welcome." Leigh smiled, always cheerful. I had a feeling she was waiting for me to leave so she could get Jada on the phone and gossip.

"Well, since you're here. What's the word from the garage?" Ian asked.

I twisted around on my seat to glance at Leigh.

"What? Oh! Okay, fine. Fine. I'll leave you guys to have your chat in peace." She sighed and abandoned her seat beside Ian. Her fat and sassy mutt remained, too obsessed with us shifter guys to leave whenever we were around. Petunia set her chin on my knee and whined until I scratched around her ears.

"Aside from Lyle being a dog shifting mutt of some kind, I don't have much to tell you. I know he deals pot and codeine to some of the customers when nobody's looking, but there hasn't even been a veiled offer toward me yet."

"That's fine. You're new, they're feeling you out, and you need to prove yourself before they'll bring you in on it. That's usually how this works."

"I know. How far am I supposed to take this?"

"Anything and everything that won't put a civilian in harm's way."

I sighed. "Okay."

Ian read me like a book, raising both brows while leaning back to fix me with a skeptical look. "What's wrong? You having second thoughts now 'cause of Jada?"

"Kinda… I don't want to fuck things up with her."

"As soon as this job is done, you're free to tell her everything. We can come clean to the entire town, Hunt, and her family. He'll love you to death then."

"Yeah, I know. Nadir already coached his family on what not to say, so my cover should be fine."

"Take off this weekend with Jada. You need to look like an everyday Joe. Get out of town and get back to it Monday."

"Gotta love a drug-dealing asshole who doesn't open on Sundays," I quipped. "God forbid we all do some work on a Sunday, but selling some meth to that guy around the corner? Nothing wrong with it."

"We don't have solid proof Tito's involved yet."

"He's gotta be. I'm telling you, it's him."

"Get us the proof we need and we'll take him down."

~

What are you doing this weekend? I Swype'd on my phone to her.

Jada's answering text hit me an hour later.

Jada: *Sorry. I'm hanging out with my parents and Dad bitches if he thinks I'm talking to you now.*

Me: *It's no problem.*

Jada: *I don't have anything to do this weekend. I thought about working at the spa.*

Me: *What about letting me take you out somewhere?*

Jada: *What do you have in mind?*

Me: *It's summer, so how about a day at the beach?*

Jada: *I don't have a swimsuit.*

Me: *Buy one. I hear Amazon has free two-day shipping.*

y phone rang a second later, the lit screen revealing Jada's name and number. "Missed the sound of my voice?" I teased her.

"Seriously? Buy a swimsuit online?" Laughter and exasperation filled her voice in equal measures.

"Why not?"

"I have to try stuff on."

"We can hit up a store on the way out then." I pictured her prancing in and out of a changing room for my opinion on increasingly skimpy swimsuits.

Fuck. Yes.

"Fine. What time will we leave?"

"If we're on I-45 by eight, we'll have time to stop at the department store of your choice and get lunch somewhere on the island."

"Sounds like a deal."

I worked hard throughout the week, and by Saturday, I couldn't wait to spend time with Jada for more than a few passing minutes at the spa or a stolen hour during the evening.

On the day of our trip, I was up with the dawn, showered, and had my change of clothes crammed into a backpack. I stepped out of my house to find Jada's Camry waiting for me. She leaned against the driver's door, her ebony hair free against her shoulders. A dress in earth-toned colors complemented her skin in shades of gold, topaz, and brown, and the wedge sandals on her feet bumped her up close to my height.

"Did you seriously drive here to leave your car in my driveway?"

"Yeah." Her eyes crinkled at the corners. "Give the neighbors something to whisper about. Plus, I wanted to surprise you with these." She reached into the passenger seat and removed two white boxes. The sweet smell of fresh goods from the bakery hit my sensitive nose before she raised the lid.

"You're amazing."

"I know," she replied, grinning. "I brought coffee, too."

"Marry me," I teased.

If only there was a way for her to understand

how much I meant it. From the moment we met alongside the highway, I had become hers and knew there'd never be another woman for me. It transcended a lust for her in the physical sense; I respected her wit, humor, and drive to transform her business into a booming success.

"I try not to get hitched on the third date," Jada quipped back.

A few minutes into the drive, she passed me a still-warm breakfast sandwich—melted cheese on egg with bacon, stuffed between a flaky croissant. We sipped coffee and chatted about everything but her dad's disdain for me.

"God, I love your car."

"Thanks."

"I can't believe you have a movie player."

"You can put something in if you want to. Otherwise, I'm gonna talk you to death." Or rather, ask her too many questions and possibly put her off. I couldn't help it, but I wanted to know everything about her I could learn. "The case is in the center console."

"Maybe after my hands aren't so sticky."

A glance at Jada revealed our box of snacks had emptied. She'd brought two donuts for each of us, and I'd polished mine off in the first fifteen minutes of our drive. "Where's the woman who ate with me at Lottie's?"

"Huh?" She peeked around at me, donut frosting clinging to her lower lip and corner of her mouth.

"You know, the girl who's watching her sugar." I reached over and wiped a bit of glaze from her chin.

"I guess I figured if you really like me, I can be myself."

"Good." That's all I wanted.

And she was all I needed.

~

*W*e hit up a mall outside of Houston. Unfortunately, Jada didn't put on a fashion show and kept her purchase a mystery, hustling her goods to the counter before I could catch more than a hint of her chosen color. Damn. My patience was rewarded when she stepped out from the changing room at the waterpark.

Maybe I was accustomed to being around the wrong kind of girl, but I expected her to exit in a single piece, her curvy body hidden beneath an over-sized cover-up.

Jada proved me wrong when she strolled out in a bikini. The black bottoms hugged her ass and full hips, drawing my attention to her thick thighs. She had muscle beneath the soft flesh associated with being a bigger girl. I fantasized about peeling it off of her with my teeth until my eyes locked on her cleavage.

"Holy shit."

Jada paused mid-stride, her confidence visibly wavering on the precipice, caught on a treacherous divide between fearless and uncertain. "Is it ugly?" The unspoken question in her eyes made me want to pound whoever came before me responsible for the doubt she displayed. *Am I too fat for this?* Someone always put those kinds of thoughts into a woman's head. Someone had made her insecure.

"No." I shook my head quickly. "Not at all." I covered the distance between us in two steps, and without giving her the chance to argue, I cupped Jada's cheeks with both hands and kissed her. "You're beautiful."

I didn't give a damn what anyone around us thought; I kissed her again, aware of the men checking out her round ass.

Then I kissed her one more time for the women watching me to leave no doubt in Jada's mind that she was the only one who mattered. I had eyes for her, and only her.

"C'mon," I said as we parted and twined our fingers.

She leaned into me as I took a step back, her eyes glassy, seeming not to realize the kiss was over and it was time to walk from the changing area.

"You okay?"

"Huh?" She snapped out of it. Her dark eyes darted left and right then fixed to me. "I'm fine."

If she felt even a fraction of the desire and unbearable need coursing through me, then I knew exactly how she felt.

"Wipe that smug grin off your face."

I flattened my expression, internally pulling on my Ian impersonation. Nobody could surpass that mean bastard's solemn stares once he was pissed off. Leigh didn't believe us, but she was fortunate to never see that side of him.

"You're such a smart-ass," Jada fussed. Despite her words, a grin raised the corners of her mouth.

We spent the day daring each other onto the highest slides. When the lines grew too long, we chose to lazily float along the tube river that wound through the entire park.

"I'm hungry. Are you hungry?"

"Well…"

"Baby, we've been out in the sun all day and ain't had a bite since those donuts."

So I talked her into abandoning her diet again for the weekend. We ate BBQ from the concession stand

and shared an Oreo and ice cream funnel cake. Since she'd left her credit card in her locker, and mine was stashed in the zip-up pocket of my board shorts, she finally let me catch the entire bill.

If only she knew how much money I had. On top of bringing in a ton of cash from my detail shop, I earned money hand over fist anytime Ian set up work for us overseas. If we didn't come close to clearing half a mil each year, he wasn't doing his job.

The amount of money he'd paid me for going into prison was obscene, enough to make up for having to dance around with my dick out every time a guard thought I had some contraband tucked under my balls or something.

"This has been really fun. I'm glad you talked me into coming."

"It doesn't have to end, you know. We can grab a room and hit up the aquarium or something tomorrow. Laser tag, maybe."

"A room?" Jada leaned back on her seat and stared at me.

"Separate rooms. Kind of a waste of money though, don't you think?"

"Feeling that lucky, huh?"

I grinned. "Nah, nothing like that. Men and women can sleep in the same room without having sex." Contrary to my comment, I struggled to keep my eyes above her generous bust line. "*I* can anyway."

"It is a longish drive back…"

"C'mon. It'll be fun." My motivations were selfish. I wanted more time with her, away from gossips and prying eyes. Out here, I could be myself for the most part. Jada got to see the real me, a guy who loved the water and having fun.

~

JADA

*A*fter choosing an overpriced Motel 8 room for the night, we settled on sharing a meat lover's pizza with all the works and cans of lemonade from the vending machine. Taylor was the worst kind of influence.

Women like Dani didn't consider me to be too large, but when I sat down, my thighs spread and my tummy developed three distinct rolls. My breasts were too large for my frame — they may look amazing in a bikini or a corset, but the reality is shoulder pain, expensive bras, and tailored clothes.

Lacking anything to wear but my breezy summer dress, I'd convinced him to at least let me run into the Family Dollar to pick up cheap sweats and a t-shirt for the night. I had the first shower, emerging afterward in my unflattering navy blue sweats and oversized men's tee. Taylor wolf whistled then moved past me.

I listened for the sound of the shower and lay back on one of the two queen beds. An overactive imagination treated me to visuals of Taylor in the steaming stall, all bare skin and hard muscle without the interruption of his swim trunks.

Was he thinking about me, too? Hard cock in his hand, pumping and fantasizing about being inside me instead?

Fuck, I hoped so.

Then why can't I have sex with him tonight? So what if it's only the third date?

Because he was just in prison a month ago and probably has who-knows-what, the insidious voice of reason whispered into my thoughts.

But we could use a condom! My naughty shoulder angel attempted to convince me.

But you don't have one, said my devilish conscience.

Damn. And if he had one, I'd be freaked out and wondering why he came equipped to a beach date.

Everything about Taylor struck me as too good to be true, a thought confirmed when he stepped from the restroom with a white hotel room towel around his shoulders. Close-fitting, white boxer-briefs clinging against the chiseled muscle of his upper thighs, a black band low on his lean hips. His swim trunks hadn't been so tiny, so insignificant, or so fucking tight. I swallowed and raised my eyes away from his bulge.

"Wanna check out the sights and take a ferry ride before we hit the road tomorrow?"

My mind went to dirty, dirty places. *Oh yeah, I have some sights for you to see.*

"Jada?"

"Hmm? Oh!" I snapped out of my naughty little fantasy. "Yeah, sounds like a plan. We could drive around and check out all the tree sculptures."

"And eat at Joe's."

"You are so food focused," I said, laughing at the dreamy expression on his face.

"What can I say? I love seafood."

His heart-melting, crooked grin made me clench with desire, dampening my brand new cotton panties.

"Night, sweet cheeks."

The endearment made me roll my eyes, but I smiled. "Goodnight."

Long after Taylor was muffling his snores into the pillow, I remained awake in the adjacent bed, cursing my self-imposed chastity. Lisa would have slept with him after the first date for sure, regardless of the criminal record attached to him.

I wasn't her, and waiting would make the actual sex that much sweeter if we did come to it.

Confident in my choice, I rolled over and went to sleep.

7

JADA

I argued with my dad over the course of a week during occasional squabbles at dinnertime. He claimed I chose a hoodlum over him, and I accused him of butting into my life.

"Do you know how it looks when people see you at that place? Do you know how it makes me look?" he had asked.

"Daddy," I'd said in an exasperated voice. I didn't want conflict; I wanted to tell him about the feline protector who occasionally showed up at my place. "I go to take my boyfriend a freaking Aquafina and a brownie at lunch. Hell, half of the force goes there for their lube jobs!"

"I don't," he'd grumbled.

"I'm not saying they don't have some bad habits,

or that Tito isn't up to no good, but the work is great."

My excuses hadn't soothed my ruffled father. If anything, he became more aggressive and finally talked a warrant out of the judge. The search was a bust, making him the laughingstock of Quickdraw for a solid week. Any time I went into the supermarket or stopped for gas, I heard whispers about it.

Mom blamed me, so I stopped showing up for family dinner until she phoned one Friday morning.

"Let's go away tonight, Jada."

"Go where?" I asked, guarded.

"Does it matter where? You never find the time to come out with me anymore. I'm the doctor, but I still find time to spend with you."

Mom's unintentional guilt trip resulted in me dropping all plans for the weekend. I left the shop in Lisa's capable hands, smooched Taylor, and left Friday afternoon for a drive into downtown Houston with my mother.

"What has happened to us, Jada? Why did I have to shame you into coming with me for the weekend, when you went away with your new boyfriend only a little while ago?"

I sighed. "I knew this was coming. This is what happened to us, Mom. Whether I come to hang out with you voluntarily or not, I know you're going to lecture me about my life choices. Because I'm not another doctor like you and Granddad. You guys don't do this to Danny."

My mother was a beautiful woman, a thinner, older version of me with her dark hair cut into an angled bob. All my life, she'd forced me onto one diet after another, wanting the perfect little girl.

"I only wanted the best for you," she said in a low voice.

"I know," I replied.

In under thirty minutes, our drive had become awkward, and I was trapped for at least another hour before we reached our destination. I sank against the door and stared out the window again at the strips of outlet stores bordering the highway.

"When I came to this country, I knew I wanted to help people. I had an amazing new chance given to me and wanted to use it to the fullest. So I became a doctor."

"I know, Mom…" I sighed when I-45's traffic slowed to a standstill, placing us in bumper-to-bumper conditions. Make that two hours before we arrived.

"This time I am telling it to you for a different reason."

"Not because I've shamed you by becoming an overpriced beautician?" I asked. The bitter question left my lips, regretted in an instant. "Sorry," I whispered, quieting.

My mother didn't answer. She focused her eyes on the rear of the truck ahead of us. Her brown eyes narrowed.

"I'm sorry," I repeated.

"No. I deserved that. Your life is yours to do with as you choose. I complain often about what you do wrong, but I never tell you what you've done that is right. I *am* proud, Jada. You turned that ugly little building into something beautiful where women will happily throw their money at you. Perhaps you are not healing bodies in the operating room, but you are healing spirits. That is just as important."

Tears pricked at my eyes, threatening to overflow and send me into a cryfest. A few blinks pushed them back.

"Thanks, Mom. That means everything to me."

"This boy of yours needs your help, too," she told me.

"Help him to what?"

"Help him to stay on a good, law-abiding path. Prove your father wrong."

I sighed and twisted the ends of my hair around my finger. "From everything I can tell, Mom, he's on the straight and narrow. Just because he works at Tito's doesn't make him a bad person."

"You know what your father thinks of that place."

"I do, but where else is a mechanic gonna work? Or is he just pissed because I'm not with someone he thinks is worthy of me?"

Mom drummed her fingers on the steering wheel and glanced over at me. "My father never approved of anything I did either, and if I'd listened to him, I wouldn't have you. I wouldn't have left India. You were never a mistake, Jada. You and Danny are the joy of my life and you've been worth every struggle I encountered since leaving home.

This time I couldn't hold back the tears. They leaked down my face, so I swiped at my cheeks and searched for a tissue in my purse.

"Makeup ruined," I muttered between sniffles.

"You're pretty without it," she replied. "I know you think I'm hard on you, but I just want you to be happy, sweetheart."

My mom had found an awesome place where aspiring artists could buy canvases, chat with their fellow customers, and create works of art while nibbling treats from the snack bar. We arrived just in time to join an instructor-led class.

We painted for most of the evening and drank too much, sharing a bottle of red velvet wine between us. Later, we walked arm in arm to the Cheesecake Factory where we sobered up over hot sandwiches and delicious, fattening desserts. For the first time in all of my life, Mom didn't chastise me about my dinner choices.

As we were both unwilling to undertake the long drive back to Quickdraw after an evening of wine-sipping and good food, we found a nearby hotel and checked in for a night.

Dad called just as I finished brushing out my hair from the shower.

"Hey, punkin. Is it World War III yet?" he asked.

"*Dad.*"

"What? I wanted to check in on my favorite girls and make sure everything was okay."

"We're having fun," I admitted. I sat on the edge of the bed in my nightshirt while Mom showered.

"That's good. I'm real glad to hear it." He fell quiet, as if he didn't know what to say next.

If I could make peace with Mom, I could definitely make amends with Daddy. I dragged in a deep breath and swallowed my pride.

"I love you, Daddy. I'm sorry we've been fighting. I wasn't trying to embarrass you."

My dad paused. "I'm sorry, too, Jada. I don't mean to butt into your life."

"I know you don't. Can we at least agree to disagree about Taylor?"

"All right," he answered, surprising me.

"Really?"

"Really. I can't say I trust him yet. I still plan to keep an eye on the kid, but I'll lay off of you. Anyway, I didn't call to take up all your time. Enjoy the weekend with your mama."

"I will. Love you," I repeated again, smiling.

"Love you, too."

I ended the call and found an unanswered text from Taylor, forgotten while out with my mother. We made plans to meet after Sunday dinner with my family, and then I set the phone down on the bedside table just as Mom emerged from the bathroom.

"Who were you talking to?"

"Dad called to check up on us. He sends his love and said to have fun."

"With Danny leaving for the Army soon, he worries, is all. Did you two have a nice chat?" Mom settled behind me with a brush and stroked the bristles through my thick hair. I watched her reflection in the mirror to see her admiring the golden brown ombre coloring the lower portion.

"Yeah, we did. Mostly. He said he'll lay off some."

"That's something, at least." She set the brush aside and began braiding my hair. "Speaking of which, I saw your former jailbird."

"*Mom.* He has a name."

She chuckled and nudged the ticklish spot above

my hip with her fingers. "I know his name is Taylor," she supplied without waiting for me to offer. "He's very polite, and... incredibly handsome. You certainly have good taste where looks are concerned."

"You met him?" I twisted around to look at her.

"I may have needed an oil change. Anyway, what I wanted to say was I'm sorry for judging him before we met. He's a nice young man, and you have my support. Your father will come around in time."

She was right. As the next two weeks passed, my dad made a visible effort to cool his jets about Taylor dating me. If he still disapproved, he didn't show it, and the tension at home gradually eased.

As for Taylor, he wasn't what I expected. He was interested in the simplest forms of entertainment. Indoors, we enjoyed peaceful evenings in front of video games and watched movies, my cheek against his chest. Outside, he cheerfully suggested fun activities for couples like horseback riding, hiking in Sam Houston State Park, and rock wall climbing at the activity center.

"You don't want to go drinking or dancing?" I asked, dubious.

"I can drink at home, and I don't dance," he muttered. "What, you wanna go dancing?"

"No, I hate dancing."

"Then…" He gave me a puzzled look. "Why are we talking about dancing?"

"I'm trying to figure you out, is all." I stopped to lean against a tree by the path, winded from the uphill walk. We were in the final days of summer. Cotton clung against my sweat-dampened skin and the hair at my nape was wet. The smell of the trees and earth surrounded us. I inhaled the scent of clean grass and earth, the woodlands as soothing as an evening in *Nirvana*.

"Okay, instead of trying to figure me out, why don't you try asking?"

"Why don't you do any of the things the rest of your homeboys at Tito's enjoy doing?"

"You mean wander up and down the street like I don't have any damned sense?" He barked out a quiet laugh.

I chuckled, too, and ducked my head, cheeks warm. "I always see them smoking outside the bar or hogging the basketball court."

"I had enough of the basketball court while locked up," he said dryly. "I hang out with them sometimes, Jada, but if this is your roundabout way of asking if I'm into their other activities — I'm not."

"I wasn't implying…" I bit my lower lip and shyly peeked up to find Taylor's smile remained. "So, you really like the outdoors, huh?"

"Don't you?"

"Erm…" I tugged at the neck of my t-shirt and fanned air against my skin. "I'm sweating for you, so that must mean something," I quipped. "And I guess it is nice to escape the spa for a while to enjoy the fresh air."

Taylor's bright blue eyes and charismatic smiles *also* made the experience enjoyable. Gazing into them, I melted and my breath caught in my throat. One of his hands settled at my hip, sliding up and down over the loose-fitting brown sweats I'd worn to protect my legs from the mosquitoes.

The undeniable sexual appeal he exuded had become a pervasive presence, always simmering beneath the surface whenever he touched me. His touch was electric, sneaking upward to the band of my bottoms and beneath my shirt, fingertips gliding over the strip of bare skin.

"Of course, there's a bonus to being out here with you," he said, dipping down to place a line of kisses from my neck to my ear. His teeth closed around my earlobe for a playful nibble, weakening my knees.

"What's that?"

"I get you to myself, with no one else around."

"Well…" I lifted my arms to circle his neck. "You don't have to steal me away outdoors to be alone with me."

"Sure I do." His grin widened. "No signal out here. Well, a crappy one at least. No dads, brothers, moms, or friends butting in. Just you and me."

"You're awfully patient for a man who's been in prison," I murmured. Feeling playful, I teased with a movement of my hips. It placed pressure on his cock, molding my body to the obvious outline. It turned me on to know he was as hard for me as I was wet for him, my panties damp and uncomfortable beneath my outdoors attire.

"It's a gift," Taylor replied, his husky voice a low, sensual utterance in the quiet forest.

In a move that was pure evil, Taylor adjusted his position enough to wedge his hand between us. He cupped my pussy over the layers of clothing and returned my previous tease. Every knead and pet applied indirect contact to my clit. I gasped and rolled my hips against it, eager for more.

"Like that, don't you?"

I made a quiet sound in my throat and nodded. My head fell back and my eyes shut as I surrendered to his talented fingers, bold and unhurried. Pressure built in my core, and all I could imagine was having his cock in my hands, feeling the hot flesh beneath my touch and stroking him before he entered my body to become coated in my slickness.

"How long have you wanted me?" Taylor asked.

His words, a seductive and warm breath, heated my cheek. "I can feel how wet you are through your sweats. You're fucking soaked."

"Since..." The breath hitched in my lungs. I moaned softly, eager for more, but his fingers retreated and left me wanting. "Taylor..."

"How long?" he repeated. He inhaled as if he could smell my arousal.

"Since the car ride. Since you gave me a ride to Houston. You were so sexy in your stained jeans and t-shirt." He gave a little of what I wanted, his hand over my mound without delving beneath my clothes. "I want your fingers inside me."

"I don't think I can stop myself at just my fingers, baby." His deep voice, smooth as silk, caressed my senses and made me putty in his hands. I trembled and turned my head to find his mouth and capture his lips in a kiss. As his tongue advanced into my mouth, I sucked the tip.

"You don't have to." I wanted him so bad. A dull ache throbbed between my thighs, unrelieved no matter how I rubbed against him. My heart raced with increasing desire while anticipation pooled in my core, a hot jolt of lust shooting right to my clit. "I don't want to wait anymore."

"Do you want a fuck now, or for me to make love to you later?" he asked.

"Damn you." I laughed in spite of myself and released a shaky exhalation. "Later. You're right. I'm not eager to roll around in fallen leaves and possible ant piles."

"Don't forget the mosquitos."

By the time we returned to Quickdraw, my thighs were killing me. I tried to imagine rolling onto Taylor in bed while my legs screamed with every flex.

"Raincheck, right?" he predicted with a grin as he slowed to a stop in front of my house.

"Yeah. When I can walk again without wanting to cry."

"Go take a bath, babe. I'll see you soon."

We parted with a kiss, and then I waved to him from the door. Taylor didn't pull away until I was inside with the door shut behind me.

Soon, I thought. In the meantime, I had my fantasies to keep me company until the perfect moment.

～

"Ugh. Bunch of thugs are hanging around outside again." Naomi peeked through the blinds on the storefront window. I was beside her with a big bucket of steaming, soapy water to scrub the window sills beneath them. I'd already mopped the floors. It was all I could do to burn the restless energy building ever since the weekend with Taylor.

"I wonder if that's why we have virtually no customers today."

"Call your dad and tell him to get out here."

I cracked open the blinds. One of the last days of Texas summer had reduced the world beyond my shop into a scorching wasteland. I'd gotten into the habit of taking cool drinks across the road to Taylor, much to Dad's displeasure.

"Are they dealing?" I asked Naomi.

"Nah, they're only standing ar—wait, wait, look. There's a car."

A beat up, ancient Caprice pulled up and idled by the curb. The passenger window rolled down and one of the kids stepped up to it. Money exchanged hands and the passenger took a small, semi-translucent plastic baggie from the peddler outside my spa.

I saw red. Before I knew what I was doing, I barged outside. The smell of exhaust assaulted me as the ugly blue sedan peeled away and around the corner. It burned my nose and made me choke.

"Hey, you guys get out of here." I crossed my arms and stared the three loiterers down.

"C'mon, baby, you don't gotta be like that." I

recognized Jared, a punk teen who used to bully kids at my brother's school.

"I'm not your baby and you're scaring off my customers. So get lost or I'm calling the cops."

"Ah man, the bitch is gonna call her pops," the smoking man swore. He tossed his cigarette to the curb and ground it under his boot. Tyrese, the oldest and a college dropout, was the son of the local florist. His mother had poured her heart out to me during a massage once, lamenting how far he'd fallen from the tree. His father worked long hours at a local prison to help support the family.

"Get *out* of here," I ordered again, "and take your butts with you. I'm not having you littering or dealing on my sidewalk."

"Bitch, it's a free country. You don't own this shit," Jared said. He'd shaved half of his blond hair to reveal the marijuana leaf tattoos on his skull. Oh, so original.

My brows rose. "Yeah?"

Turning my back on them, I marched inside my shop. Their snickers followed me. *Stupid idiots think they've run me off. I'll show them.* "That mop bucket still back there, Naomi?"

"Yeah, but—"

"Thanks."

I grabbed it and stepped outside again with the

bucket of filthy water. In one heaving thrust, I splashed its contents over them and drenched two of the boys at once. "Oops!" I cried. I splashed Tyrese and the third kid, his face unfamiliar to me. I dubbed him 'Saggy-Pants' instead.

Shouts and cries of profanity filled the air. They called out new and inventive insults I'd never heard regarding my weight and my face. If I was a weaker person, if I had less self-esteem, if I didn't have Taylor to convince me of how gorgeous I was — I'd let it bother me.

"What the fuck do you think you're doing, lady?" Saggy-Pants demanded.

"I didn't mean to splash you," I said sweetly when one of them stomped toward me with an aggressive posture. He was close enough for me to smell the sweet odor of marijuana on his skin. "I wanted to wash the butts off the sidewalk, but you stepped in my way. Oops."

Saggy-Pants raised his fist, expecting me to back down, but a wild kind of fury had taken hold and I was too far gone to turn tail. I'd brawl with him in the street if I had to; too experienced with my enormous little brother and an assload of male cousins who liked to play rough and dirty. He had another thing coming if he thought he could intimidate me in front of my own property.

"The hell is going on over here?" Taylor demanded as he jogged across the street to my rescue, a black knight in oil-stained armor. His fitted t-shirt stuck against his sweaty skin, clinging to every contour, dip, and valley of his chiseled torso. He wore his coveralls with the sleeves tied around his waist.

"Uh. Sup, man," Jared said.

"Hey, T.J.," Tyrese mumbled.

"They giving you trouble, Jada?" Taylor stepped in close beside me, slipping his arm around my waist. The smell of engine grease and sweat assaulted my nose, but I ignored it to kiss his cheek.

"Aw, shit man, is this your girl?" Jared eyed me up and down.

I was and everyone knew it. These bastards were playing dumb.

"Just cleaning out the trash, babe," I replied, gesturing toward the wet cement. Cigarette butts and gum wrappers floated in the gutter.

"We was just messin' around, T.J. No big deal, man. We're leaving," Saggy-Pants said.

I rolled my eyes. *Taylor walks up with his muscles showing and now they're all ready to hang it up and go. I can't believe this.*

"Lemme catch your asses around here bothering her again. See what happens," Taylor threatened.

"'Kay, dude, fine. Damn. Marco, c'mon, dude. We got a better place we can hang out," I overheard Tyrese saying to the one with the too-large jeans.

Their group ambled off like a pack of cubs with their tails between their legs. Once they were gone, I wriggled free and turned to face my boyfriend. "Were you keeping an eye on my shop?" I demanded.

A sheepish grin covered his face. He was unshaven, but the look suited him, dark stubble contrasting against his sandy brown skin. "Naomi used your phone to send me a text," he admitted. "I was on my way out of the shop for the day."

"I'm sorry."

"No, don't be."

"The least I can do is get you a cold drink. Come on inside for a few."

While Taylor scrubbed his hands and face in the restroom, I visited the cooler where I kept cold cans of iced tea and Cokes for my customers. I lingered in front of it, allowing the frosty air to cool my face.

"Okay, business is dead, so I'm heading out. See you tomorrow." Naomi glanced at the hallway leading to the rear of my shop then turned to me and mouthed, "Have fun."

I shoved her. She and Lisa couldn't believe I was still holding out on sex with Taylor. Maybe I was making excuses, but the time hadn't felt right again.

He'd even brought me papers from the local clinic confirming he was STD-free when I made the difficult choice and asked one awkward evening when I was leaving his place.

Why hadn't he gotten bored and moved on yet?

Naomi flipped the 'open' sign to 'closed' on her way out.

"Where'd Naomi go?" Taylor asked. He stepped from the back, drying his hands on a paper towel.

"No clients booked, so she took off to get ready for a date or something."

"In that case, mind giving me a peek over at your new space?" He gestured toward the new archway in the wall connecting the two shops. I planned to hang a beaded curtain there when everything was finished.

"Yeah, c'mon, they installed the new counters yesterday and hooked up the plumbing for the pedicure stations. The skylights are all finished, too."

When everything was said and done, I'd have six manicure tables, four pedicure stations, a new massage room, and a larger reception desk.

"It's all looking good," Taylor said.

"Thanks." I beamed, proud as a new mother. My business *was* my baby, at least for now.

"You still going for stained glass on the front windows?"

My expression fell. "No, the cost was too much, but I did find an alternative. I can get a custom film put on them which will provide the same sort of effect I wanted. I just need to decide on a pattern."

Taylor moved in front of me near the curtained windows in question and slid his hands up and down my arms. His touch ignited goose bumps, sending sparks dancing across my skin.

"Your place is locked, right?"

"Yeah, but—"

Without so much as a grunt of exertion, Taylor plucked me up and set me on the counter. Squealing the whole time, I pushed at his shoulders.

"You could have hurt your back!"

Taylor's brows rose. "Huh? Doing what?"

"Picking me up," I fussed at him. "I weigh too much for—"

He silenced me with a kiss. Taylor took his time, his tongue making a slow sweep into my mouth. His hands slid down from my hips to my thighs and encouraged them to part so his body could wedge between them. My skin broke out in goose bumps as he nudged my skirt upward until the pink, bikini cut panties beneath were visible.

One hand skated over the top of my thigh and traveled low until he found the edge of my panties.

He circled his index finger and teased me, filling my body with delicious anticipation for more.

Even when we broke away to breathe, he didn't stop. His kisses continued down my throat until I was putty in his hands, my core clenching hot and wet with need. He explored me top and bottom, teasing between my legs while fondling one breast. I moaned as he circled his thumb over a peak too prominent for my bra to conceal.

"You have the perfect pair of tits."

His mouth lowered to my breast and sealed around the nipple. He alternated between them, suckling through my shirt to leave two wet spots against the floral patterned fabric. Too bad I'd left my piercings forgotten beside my bathroom sink.

Taylor continued his downward path until his hot breath washed over the thin cotton covering my slit. They were already damp, a damning beacon of my desire for him. He licked me playfully through the fabric.

"Fuck," I swore on a moaned breath.

His fingers slipped beneath my panties and found me, my body so wet, so receptive for him, that two digits slid to the knuckle without resistance. I couldn't form words, only a weak groan.

Maybe it hadn't been about waiting for the right moment. Maybe I'd needed him to do this, to take charge. I shuddered and involuntarily clenched around his fingers, the edges of a potential orgasm teasing past my senses.

"Open your shirt."

I did it with a trembling hand, barely able to focus. He was doing things, *amazing things* to me, robbing me of concentration.

"You're stunning, Jada. I could kiss every inch of you and never grow tired of it."

"Why don't you?" I asked, breathless.

"Because I plan to occupy my mouth in other ways."

Taylor dragged my panties from beneath me with confident, firm tugs, and then they were hanging by one of my ankles, my pussy bared to him. With my thighs spread, he saw every inch from my perfect Brazilian wax to the piercing snuggled against my hood.

His breath caught in his throat. He hadn't expected that.

"Do you like it?"

His answer came without words, produced by the touch of his tongue against the small piece of metal. A jolt of electric pleasure sparked across my skin, clenching my core.

"I've been wanting a taste since the first moment I saw you," he murmured. His warm breath ghosted over my wet skin.

Trembling, I raised a hand to my breasts. They felt tight and tender inside the pushup bra. "Don't tease me."

A slow, upward lick parted my folds. From that moment, Taylor ignored my clit and kept me in suspense by focusing on every other inch of my slick nether lips. My thighs quivered and my toes curled in my sandals until one plopped to the floor.

"Taylor," I gasped out, taking him by the shoulders with both hands.

His tongue dipped within my slick passage, creating flutters in my stomach. Firm, strong fingers ran upward along my thighs, then cupped my ass and dragged me forward another inch.

"Better than any dessert." He blew a cool stream of air across my sensitive flesh.

With one hand remaining on my hip, the other moved between my legs, Taylor slid his fingers inside me again and I instinctively clamped down around him. He chuckled and flicked his tongue over my clit as fingers noisily slapped in and out of my wet body.

"Don't worry, sweetheart. I'm not going anywhere until I'm done with you."

Taylor alternated between slow licks, sharp nips, and hungry suckles while his fingers pumped within my tight channel. He built me up, brought me to the cusp of orgasm, and then he'd turn away and kiss my thighs. The infuriating man repeated the torturous cycle until I thought I would burst.

"Please," I sobbed. "Oh God, Taylor. Please, baby, please."

Squirming and thrashing, I came while holding him in a death grip at the shoulders. With my head thrown back, I screamed his name, thrusting my hips, pushing against him, driven wild until only nonsensical words fell from my mouth.

Taylor coaxed me to lie down on the empty counter, my skirt flipped above my waist and panties dangling from one ankle. One of my legs, limp and boneless like a noodle, fell from the side of the counter.

I thought he was done.

I was wrong.

His fingers slid free from my body, replaced by his tongue. He took my limp leg and hooked it over his shoulder while he feasted on my pussy. I writhed against the stone countertop and searched for something — anything — to hold on to.

He was a sadist, skilled in the fine art of sexual torture. And I'd become his very, *very* willing victim. When he glanced up from between my legs, I saw his pupils had blown so wide, barely any blue remained.

He dipped down again and the world around me spun. Without warning, his lips sealed around my swollen clit. Just like that, I was his—exploding, lost, and convulsing on the table as another orgasm shot through me.

My second climax was merciless and more potent than its predecessor. My body was quivering, on fire, subjected to too much sensation at once. One of his hands palmed my breasts and alternated between pinching each nipple, while his tongue tip explored my pierced clit hood.

It was heaven and hell both, all at once. He left me gasping for air with my chest heaving and breasts bouncing wildly.

Soft kisses trailed their way up my trembling body. Taylor leaned over me and claimed my mouth with infinite tenderness. I tasted myself on his lips, salty and earthy, but the world around me remained hazy.

"Night, Jada."

"Ni—huh? You're going?" If I wasn't meek as a kitten, I would have tackled him to the floor. I wanted to spend time with him and had looked forward to a quiet movie on the couch. His place or mine, it didn't matter.

"Yeah. I got some stuff to do tonight. Trust me,

I'd back out if I could. Sorry," he apologized again, contrite features genuine.

I tried to snap out of it, but my legs were uncooperative. My foggy mind didn't want to make sense of my surroundings yet or accept my boyfriend had eaten me out on my brand new reception counter.

"Besides, I saw how stiff you've been moving since the hike."

Damn him for being so observant. "What about dinner tomorrow?"

"I think dinner tomorrow is great." I wanted to be angry, but he won me over with his bashful smile. "If you're feeling up to it. Don't rush on my account."

"Oo-kaay?" I dragged the word out, still frazzled and out of sorts.

"I really am sorry." Taylor chuckled, that low and sexy sound I loved so much, and leaned down to kiss my forehead. "Don't fall asleep in here or your back will scream tomorrow… and that would be a shame."

"I'm not. I won't." I hated that we weren't at his place or mine, where I could have stripped and talked him out of his plans to leave, but I appreciated his decision not to hit it for a quickie and leave. "You don't want anything?" I dropped my eyes down to his apparent erection.

He paused and glanced at me. "You offering?"

"No. Yes. Maybe," I mumbled, indecisive. "Do you have to go?"

"Baby, I'm covered in crap from rebuilding a diesel engine. Trust me. If we were anywhere else and this was any other time... Damn." He inhaled slowly and gazed down at me, smoldering desire in his eyes. I could see his arousal, the silhouette of his hard cock visible beneath his coveralls. I dared to skate my fingers over the bulge and earned a sharp hiss of his breath in response.

"Girl, you have no idea how much I wanna stay."

"No, trust me. I know."

~

TAYLOR

The timing was shit. I should have been home, making love to Jada. Instead, I was standing around for a heist.

Tito never involved me in much of the criminal side of the business. Once or twice in the month since I began working for him, they'd asked me to pass a message to one of his dealers or hold on to some product. With each request, the stakes raised a little higher.

'Don't fuck up' became my motto, until I finally

scored the big job. Without a doubt, I knew this was my chance to prove myself. This was the beginning of the end, my chance to earn a way into the inner circle and to see what his operation was really about.

He wanted us to break into the local pharmacy. It was a small, Mom and Pop kind of place owned by an elderly couple and their middle-aged daughter. Their only source of income and a business in their family for decades.

The daughter was in on it, an addiction to Vicodin driving her to help rob her own parents.

To impress Tito, I concocted a plan for her to claim she forgot to lock the back door while closing up for the evening and taking out the trash. We'd hide behind the dumpster, burst in, and take the store for everything it was worth.

We did.

I held her at gunpoint with an unloaded pistol for the camera, my identity concealed beneath a ski mask. My heart pounded inside my ribcage the entire time. I'd never pointed a gun at a civilian woman in all my life.

I hated the way it made me feel. My skin crawled and I broke out in a cold sweat. On my orders, she punched in the code to the narcotics safe, we emptied enough codeine to stone a rhino, and we bounced. After we were gone, she phoned the police to report the armed robbery.

She met up with us hours later for her share of the wealth.

"What'd the cops say, Vickie?" I lounged on an old couch we had set up in the garage.

Vickie shook out her auburn hair from her knit cap. "The usual bullshit. They took the surveillance tapes and dusted for prints. My folks are fretting and contacted their insurance."

"They don't suspect you helped?"

"Of course not. Now give me my take, man." She shifted restlessly from foot to foot.

"Keep your pants on," Lyle grunted. He worked at a table, counting out shares of the pills to divide between Tito's drug trade and the robbery participants.

"I need it, Lyle. My head is pounding and this is the only shit that works."

Lyle passed the antsy woman a black film canister. Vickie fumbled the lid off and popped two pills into her mouth. Without a further word, she gave us the bird then headed out.

"Is she always an ungrateful bitch?" I asked.

"Yeah. That's just Vee."

"You were awesome in there," a kid named Joey gushed at me. He had to be about eighteen or nineteen, and too young to be tangled up in this mess. "I can't believe Tito let you lead the entire thing."

I just laughed at him, unwilling to give any verbal encouragement.

"So, you ready for your share, T.J.?" Lyle tossed me a bottle of thirty. I threw it back.

"Nah, none for me, dawg. I never do the shit I deal with," I said with a head shake. "Bad business."

The dog shifter frowned at me. "What? You too good to get high with us, too? You don't wanna hang with us. You won't get high—"

"Sounds like a smart man," Tito commented from the doorway. He came in smoking one of his thin, black clove cigars. Flimsy tendrils of sweet scented smoke wafted from him.

"Besides, never know when my parole officer is gonna ask me to piss, you know?"

"Whatever, pussy." Lyle chuckled at his own joke. It didn't bother me in the least; my cougar would always be superior to his mangy mutt.

"Hey, Taylor, come on back into my office." Tito nodded toward the door.

I followed him, and once I was inside, the man shut the door then gestured with one beefy hand for me to take a seat. The inside of Tito's office was a pimp palace decorated with exotic fur, leather, and gold. A legitimate pimp cup stood on display at the edge of his desk, a gold goblet with his name spelled out in bling.

Once I settled in the seat opposite his desk, Tito lowered his bulk into the one behind it. He gazed at me quietly with appraising brown eyes.

"Heard you got into it earlier with Tyrese, Marco, and Jared."

I snorted. I could play it two ways, apologetic or resolute in my behavior. True to my inner nature, I chose the latter. "They were giving Jada a hard time, making a mess outside her shop, so I told 'em I'd beat their asses if they show up again."

Tito blew smoke and nodded. "I'll tell the boys to keep their business clear of your girl's place. How's that sound?"

"Sounds good, man. Thanks."

"That wasn't the only thing I needed to have a private word with you about."

This is it, I hoped. *My chance to find out the real deal behind what's going on.*

"Yeah?" I asked.

"Beer?" he countered.

"Won't say no to a cold one." Tito removed one from the mini-fridge behind his desk and slid it to me.

Condensation from the frosty Corona moistened

my fingers. I popped the cap off with my thumb and slouched back in the seat.

"So, let's skip past the bullshit and go straight to the truth. What sort of cat are you that's got Lyle's hackles all up in a shitty twist?"

I grunted and put on a show of being dismayed. "Fucker outed me like that?" It was against our unspoken shifter code of ethics to dox each other to humans. I frowned severely, suppressing the urge to leave and promptly bust Lyle in his face.

"Part of his job. He lets me know when your kind are sniffing about the place."

"Fair enough. I'm a cougar, which is partially why I came up this way. I was eager to find a place with lots of woods to run in."

Tito's eyes lit up with greed, but he quickly hid it beneath phony nonchalance.

"You the one Granny Matthews saw back there with her goats a week back?"

I rubbed the back of my neck. "I got hungry... it was late. I hunted and couldn't find shit out there." To be fair, I'd picked off an ancient member of her flock she'd mentioned wanting to put down soon anyway, and then I made sure the old lady wandered up on a few loose fifties in her yard later that day.

Tito chortled. "I guess the Micky D's after-midnight menu ain't good enough for one of y'all."

"Heh. Yeah, you got that right. Gotta let the animal roam free sometimes."

I couldn't fucking stand him. Tito was slimy, the kind of slimy that meant any self-respecting man wouldn't leave his daughter, wife, or girlfriend alone with him.

"I need somebody with your skills for this business. Lyle's loyal, but he's never gonna be anything more than a follower. I need a man with cajones. Some real smarts."

"I haven't really done anything—"

"I disagree. You chased those boys off and guarded what was yours, T.J. I need you to do the same for my operation. There's a lot of your kind — the furry and four-legged variety — moving into Quickdraw recently."

"Yeah?"

Tito took in a drag on his clove. "The sheriff who just got elected? He's one. Not sure what yet, just that he's got feathers that make Lyle sneeze."

I smirked. *Good. I should stuff feathers around the place just to set that little shit off.* The idea amused me and I was certain Ian would see the humor in it, too.

"Then there's that big redneck on the volunteer fire department."

Gotta be Russ, I thought. "Him, too? Haven't met him, but I know who you're referring to."

"Yeah." Tito rubbed his chin. "MacArthur's the troublemaker though. The other big fuck minds his business and keeps out of ours. People are more willing to cross us these days than they used to be before he came around."

"Sounds like a real Boy Scout."

"Yeah." Tito laughed then he got down to the real question. "How close are you to your girl's daddy?"

"Not at all, man. He hates me."

"Shit."

"So if you wanted me to try to get him on the payroll, you're out of luck there. I'm not even allowed in his house."

"We'll worry about Hunt later. For now, I got another job for you to do, direct from the big boss. Needs to be fast and discreet. Think you can do that?"

"Discreet is what I do, Tito."

~

Judge Fitz awakened to the press of cold steel against his balls. His wife was paying a visit to their pregnant daughter out of state, so I snuck into his home around midnight.

It took me about two minutes to disable the

home security system and pick the locks on the rear door.

As for the big golden retriever he kept in the house? It piddled on the floor and ran to hide under the table when it smelled the cougar on my skin. One growl from me guaranteed he remained there.

I made my way to the upper levels and crept down the hall toward the master bedroom. Fitz never stirred until it was too late.

"I know there's a gun under your pillow. Touch it and your dog'll be the only one with balls in this house. You got me?"

The judge trembled in his bed. "What do you want?"

"I came to deliver a message. We both got some mutual friends and they ain't cool with what's going on lately."

"I can't let all of them off. I just can't. MacArthur will become suspicious sooner or later. You don't realize how much pull he—"

"I don't care how much pull he has, old man." I tapped the knife against the crease of his thigh above his femoral artery. I heard him gulp. Fear permeated the air, seeping from his pores to drench his t-shirt and thin cotton boxers. He was petrified.

And I hated myself for doing it, even if he was a crooked official.

"All right. Tell Tito I understand. I'll do better."

I grinned and tapped the steel blade against his body again. "Good. Real good. Next time, I won't wait until your wife isn't home. I'll go visit her personally. Her and that baby girl of yours."

"No, don't!"

"Then do the job we pay you for and keep our people on the streets."

With my free hand, I reached beneath the pillow and removed his handgun.

"What are you doing?" Fitz demanded. Pressure from the knife in my other hand halted his attempt to stop me from taking his pistol.

"Can't have you shooting me in my back, now can I?"

He couldn't tell it, but I was sweating bullets under my mask, afraid he'd have a coronary while I held his jewels at knifepoint. Perspiration trickled freely down my neck until I was clear of the wilderness bordering his home.

Finally, I'd made a breakthrough.

I knew how they were getting off and back onto the street, and most importantly, I'd earned Tito's trust.

8

JADA

"Bye, Jada!" Anna called from the door. My happy customer stepped outside into the dwindling sunlight, its glow casting highlights of gold against her newly henna colored hair. I waved to her and resumed sweeping the clippings from the floor.

I beamed with pride and admired the vibrant shade.

"You did a good job there. Could Naomi do something like that to me?" Beth, another client, asked from Naomi's chair.

"Mm, well, we could, but it wouldn't be that color. Your hair is darker, so the most it'll do is add a bit of a red tint to your hair when you're in the sun."

"Oh," the woman said, disappointed.

"But if you want, we can color it today," Naomi said.

"Let's do that then. I want some real bounce to it, too, girl. Make my hair swing."

I chuckled and stooped over to sweep up the mess from the floor. I had a few more calls to make around to the rest of the local businesses in the area. I'd decided, soon after chasing the troublemaking boys from in front of my shop, that it was time for all of us to take back our neighborhood. As store owners, we couldn't wait by as passive observers to our neighborhood's deterioration.

Most of the business owners had agreed it was time to take a stand. Before, we'd been afraid to call the police for fear of making trouble. We didn't open our mouths to chase them off. I'd proven it was possible to stand up to the filth giving our town a bad name.

I saw Mrs. Keller, the young woman who owned the dog grooming salon down the road, open her door and threaten to call the police on teens making her customers uncomfortable.

I even bought No Loitering signs from the general store and passed them out as the shops were opening.

It was too early to determine if our actions would

be enough, but it was a start and better than what we'd had before.

"It's a good thing you got that system from MacArthur Security," Beth said. "Stirring the hornet's nest in town is going to upset a lot of people, Jada."

"I know, but it's worth it. Besides, I'm insured. Let's hope it doesn't come to that," I said. "And if it does, I keep a gun in my purse now."

Bells chimed from the front of the shop, signaling Lisa's arrival to the salon. I waved to her, smiling.

"Oh good, Lisa, you're here. Mrs. Hatton called and wanted to know if you could fit her two boys in this week. She wants them cleaned up before their vacation."

"Oh, yeah. I'll give her a call back and set it up." She tucked her purse away behind the counter.

"Everything okay? You seem a little distracted."

Lisa ran her fingers through her short hair and peered around the quiet room. Naomi was chatting with Beth while she applied dye to the woman's hair.

"We need to talk, Jada."

The smile dropped from my face. "Okay. Let's go into the back."

With one hand between Lisa's shoulder blades, I led her to the rear room where I kept my desk, filing cabinet, computer, and physical business documents. African violets filled a pot on the desk beside a family portrait of my parents, Danny, and me.

"What's going on?"

"You know how I mentioned my parents are having problems with my little brother recently, right?"

"Yeah?" I sat on the edge of the desk.

"Well… I caught him buying drugs today. Down at the park. I was jogging and spotted him trading cash for a baggie of weed by the recreation center."

"Oh, Lisa, I'm so sorry."

She forced a faint, thin smile. "I caught up to his dumb ass and took it from him. Threatened to tell Mom and Dad. He said some not so nice things and took off. But, that's not what I wanted to talk to you about."

"What then?"

"It's about *who* was selling to him."

~

TAYLOR

uickdraw's only recreation center was positioned beside a small park, the brand new playground equipment recently

funded by Ian's generous donations. It was a favored position for illicit activities, so I hunkered down beside the center's doors with my hands in my pockets.

"Sup, T.J."

I glanced up at the approaching teen, a repeat customer I'd peddled to twice since Tito asked me to begin distributions. His freckled face made me feel like I was selling to a child.

"Fifty bucks, kid. Take it or leave it. You want quality shit then you pay quality price."

"What? That's twice the price from last week."

"Don't like it? Go buy that sorry shit from the Dixie Quarters and risk smoking Windex with it, too."

"Man, a buddy told me he heard they cut their weed with oregano and shit."

I snorted back a laugh. "You heard right. So pay up or get out of here."

"Whatever," the kid mumbled. He thumbed some bills out of his wallet and passed them over, taking an envelope in exchange.

"I don't fucking believe you," a quiet, female voice seethed behind me.

My heart leapt into a slamming rhythm, the noise of my pulse drowning out all other sound. *No*, I thought, panicked.

I glanced from my customer and into the wide brown eyes of my girlfriend, my future mate, and the woman I loved more than my own life. *No, not now.*

"Jada, wait."

Jada spun on her heel and stormed down the sidewalk. I'd be lucky to catch her before she reached her car. My customer smirked and tucked his score into his pocket.

"No. Screw you," she raged at me.

"It's not how it looks, baby, I swear."

"Oh really? Because it looks crystal clear to me." She jerked her arm from my loose grip.

"Woman, give me a fucking chance to explain."

"What kind of explanation is there for it? I didn't want to believe it, you know. I didn't want to believe Lisa when she told me she saw you selling to her *brother*. I wanted to give you the benefit of the doubt and think better of you."

I couldn't lose her. Not after everything we'd shared together, and not when I was so close to finally attaining the peace Russ and Ian received from their mates.

If I didn't come clean to Jada now, I risked losing her forever. Fuck the mission. None of it was worth anything if I lost her.

"Jada, please, give me ten minutes. After that, if

you never want to see me again, I swear I'll walk away and never bother you."

"I'll give you five."

"Can we get in your car at least so nobody over-hears all of this? It's serious."

Jada humored me and climbed into the driver's seat. I joined her in the other side and twisted to face her. "I don't really have a criminal record."

"Bullshit. I saw it and read a whole yard of crap you've done." She fired up the engine and tore out of the parking lane down from the rec center. I watched her troubled features as she focused on the road.

"It's phony. Made up stuff our digital expert created to make a paper trail. My real name is Taylor Morrison. I retired from the U.S. Army four years ago to open a mechanic shop in Houston. I've spent the past seven months of my life undercover to help out a close friend of mine with the shit going down in this town."

Jada gaped at me. "Seriously. *That's* the story you came up with?"

"It's true, every word. Ian asked me to do it because nobody around Quickdraw would know my face. Baby, I've never so much as smoked a joint in all my life. I was in the Army for over twenty years.

If I tested hot on a piss test, I would have lost my career."

"Wait. Ian? You mean Sheriff Ian MacArthur?"

"Yeah. Leigh's husband and my commanding officer."

"So you're doing what, exactly?"

"There's a whole lot to it that I can't talk about, but what I can tell you is that I don't like peddling drugs to anybody, but it's a necessity right now if I want them to trust me and think I'm one of *them*. If you don't believe me, you can ask Ian *and* Leigh. Dani and Russ, too."

"I've talked to Dani about you. She never mentioned knowing you."

"Call and ask her again," I pleaded. "What do you have to lose, Jada? Just call."

"Fine." Without looking at me again, Jada suddenly hit the brakes and turned off the main street onto an old dirt road. The car jittered and bounced as she sped over railroad tracks, then we came to an abrupt stop. "And if they don't verify your story?" she asked while taking out her phone.

"They will," I insisted.

A moment later, Russell's distinct, southern drawl greeted her with a warm welcome.

"Hi, Russ. I need to talk to Dani—no, wait. You're just as good. I want to talk to *you*."

I listened to her end of the conversation, anxiety rolling through my gut.

"I busted your friend Taylor selling dope by the rec center. Anything you wanna tell me about this?" she demanded.

Come on, Russ. Don't let me down, man.

"Really? 'Cause he says he knows you and you'd vouch for him."

She was silent on the phone for a long while, making the occasional acknowledging grunt. Several times her gaze flickered toward me, but I couldn't read her. My stomach twisted and each breath squeezed my chest just a little tighter.

"Thanks, Russ. Please tell Dani I'll see her for lunch tomorrow as planned." She ended the call and set her phone in the center console between our seats. "First Sergeant Taylor Morrison," she murmured. Her throaty, humorless laugh twisted the knife in my heart and dashed my hopes of an easy reconciliation. "You fucking liar."

"Jada, I'm sorry from the bottom of my heart for lying to you. I never thought I'd meet someone like you while doing this."

"So was I just a part of your cover? Flirt with the shop owner across the street?"

"No, it's nothing like that. When I helped you out alongside the road, I didn't know who you were. I didn't know anyone in this town except for my friends. What I did know was I couldn't let you walk away until this was done. I had to get to know you."

"All of this has been a lie... I don't even know you. How can I separate the bullshit you've told me from what's true?"

"I'm still the same guy who took you out to the splash park. The guy who likes laser tag and rock wall climbing. Nothing's changed about me but the kind of work I do."

"You're still dealing drugs."

"Not because I want to do it, but because I have to do this. Look, baby, I can't tell you everything. It's for your protection more than anything else. Ian's asked me to do this with the full authority of the governor. No one else is allowed to know because of the danger involved."

"Trying to find the root of the problem in town," she murmured, gaze on her lap.

"Right. Do you remember Dennis James?"

"Who doesn't? He used to be a nice guy until he got involved in dealing. He and my little brother, Danny, used to play ball after school. He taught him to dunk."

"I found out someone murdered him over this shit, Jada. Whoever he was working for got to him all the way in prison, and it's not going to end there unless we do something to stop it."

"Does this really change things?" Her brown eyes watched me, filled with emotion.

"Give me another chance," I pleaded again. "I'm trusting you to keep this secret between us because I care about you and I don't want this to end."

"Okay," she whispered.

I leaned across the armrest to kiss her, only for Jada to meet me halfway. Her lips parted, yielding access to her mouth and the chance to stroke my tongue against hers.

"You forgive me?"

She drew back then nibbled my lower lip in response. "This time. God, that's so hot that you're undercover."

"Hot?"

"Yes." Her fingers walked over my bulge and teased, making the hard dick beneath the denim flex in response. "My father is going to hate you if he catches you dealing," she whispered between kisses. "So you better not disappoint either of us by getting caught again."

"I won't," I promised. "But you can't utter a word of this to him. I'm sorry I put you in this position."

Her fingers rubbed over my dick through my

jeans. "I guess I'll have to be a rebellious daughter for now."

I tried to ignore the unbearable tension until her fingers snapped the button and my zipper descended. In the outdoors privacy provided by the abandoned rail station, we had no witnesses and were free to behave as we wanted. I groaned as she took me in her hand and lowered her lips to the tip.

"Fuck," I groaned as my head fell back. "This isn't how I imagined getting into your pants, Jada."

"Lucky you, then."

I tried to protest, but was promptly silenced when she drew the tip into her mouth. Her plump lips sealed around the head and I was lost to the sensation.

Jada knew what she was doing. Her tongue teased around my flared crown then wiggled over the turgid length, tracing the pulsing veins and leaving glistening trails in her wake. Before I could utter a word of encouragement, she thrust her head down and bobbed in place, making obscene, incredibly sexy slurping sounds while her tongue moistened every inch.

Fisting my fingers in her hair, I guided her down and up in time with slow pelvic thrusts. "Fuck, baby. Yes. Get all of it."

She came close. No woman had ever deep-throated

me before or even tried. Jada took me in until I experienced the tight squeeze at the back of her throat, where the angle hindered her from traveling farther. She hummed, and the vibrations made me swear out loud.

JADA

It wasn't like he'd lied about having a kid, or lied about where he'd been with the boys. He'd lied because of a job for the government, because he'd been tasked with saving our little town. My home.

The sexy truth of it made me wet until all I wanted was to touch myself. Or have him buried between my thighs, plunging his hard cock into my pussy.

I hated liars, but Taylor had earned a well-deserved pass.

"I'm close, baby. I'm close," he groaned.

Taylor laced his fingers into my hair and guided me along, pumping faster each time my mouth came closer to meeting his balls. I had him at my mercy, writhing in the car seat and practically panting for breath.

When I slid back and let his cock fall from between my lips, his disapproving moan made me smile. I was so hungry for him I could barely stand it. My thighs pressed together, panties soaked from the anticipation.

"No, wait. What are you doing?" he asked.

Now the tables are turned, I thought, delighted by the reversed roles.

I giggled at his breathless words. "If I let you come now, I'll have to wait for you to be ready again to fuck me. And like I said, I want you *now*. I won't wait or take another raincheck." Kissing the mushroomed head, I flicked my tongue against the small slit for a taste of his pre-cum. His dick was as long and thick as I'd imagined, soon glistening at its tip with another clear drop.

"Here?" he asked.

"Here. Right now."

Taylor didn't question it again. Instead, he dragged me into his lap and onto his erection. With a little wriggle, I placed myself in the perfect position, my panties the only barrier between us.

He ruined them with one tear, ripping the seam at one hip then the other; then he tossed the useless rag aside. With my skirt gathered up around my waist, I was bared to him again for the second time, my jet curls neatly groomed, trimmed down and waxed to a perfect strip above the hard cock jutting from his pelvis. His cock twitched, proving how much he appreciated the sight and making me glow with pride.

"Do we need a...?"

"I'm on the pill," I whispered, answering an unspoken question I saw in his eyes. "Do *you* think we need a condom, Sergeant? Do you trust *me* to be clean this time?"

His hip movement answered, nudging his cock between my glistening folds. I took over by directing the tip to my entrance. Then I slid it through the moisture gathered between the silken, pink lips. Groaning, he watched me through half-shut eyes.

"You're so big," I breathed out loud, surprised by the tight fit.

Needing him too much to be daunted by the size, I lowered in slow increments, drawing it out as a tease. We both groaned in mutual enjoyment. Then Taylor bucked upward and speared me in two quick strokes. His thick girth pressed into my body, parting my swollen lips until the delicious stretch was over and he'd filled my greedy channel completely. His cock seemed to go on forever.

"Oh fuck," I whispered.

Somehow, we rocked to a perfect fit. With his hands on my hips, his fingers curved around to my cheeks and spread them apart. A bump of his pelvis introduced me to the last inch, pressing my clit against his pubic bone.

"God, you're so tight."

"And you feel amazing," I breathed while undulating my hips. The enclosed confines made things a little more difficult, but I'd meant what I said. I wanted him. *Needed* him. Going home to a bedroom wasn't an option.

Taylor shoved my blouse up and fumbled with my bra. He took one look at my pierced nipples and swore under his breath. The moment he claimed my breast in his mouth, I clenched around him, earning another pleased groan and a flex of the cock filling my body. I giggled as he reached down to adjust the seat back, reclining it to give us more room. It wasn't a bed, but it was our moment. A perfect moment of passion, intense longing, and mutual need given satisfaction.

"You're beautiful, Jada. I know I've said it before, but damn, girl."

"Say it as much as you like," I replied.

Taylor's hands squeezed my ass and jerked my body in close each time I drew away. With him beneath me, I maintained most of the control over the speed of our lovemaking, and I loved every second of having him under my spell. My hips rose and fell, unrushed despite his attempt to urge me faster. My tight sheath flexed around him, squeezing and constricting to my timed movements until his eyes rolled back and his breaths quickened.

"You like that, baby? I wanna hear you come."

Taylor groaned in response before leaning forward to reclaim my tits. He nipped my left breast then gave the other the same treatment. The tiny circles he traced with his tongue jostled the horizontal barbells through my nipples and sent riveting shocks dancing up and down my spine.

Groaning, his mouth fell away from my bosom, and one hand gripped my face. Taylor kissed me hard, our tongues twisting together in a sensual dance interrupted only by our erratic breaths. My pulse became a frenzy, every muscle tensed as my trembling core tightened around him.

My climax rushed over me, a crashing wave of pleasure enhanced by his exploring fingertips. One found my clit and teased, intensifying the moment into a white-hot explosion.

I couldn't move. I was paralyzed by the sensation, crying out and gasping for breath in quick pants. Taylor took over without missing a beat, hammering away at me, my pussy so slick with juices it dripped down to his heavy balls.

Penetrative sex never made me come. Usually, I had to help it along with a vibrator. Taylor had me there before he even touched me with his hands. I shuddered and clenched around him again as his creamy warmth flooded me. His guttural groan of relief sounded like a growl in the close quarters.

"That was the best," I murmured against his cheek as we both began to come down.

"I don't wanna move."

"Me either."

We didn't. The first hour or so after our love-making was spent touching each other, our fondling interspersed with occasional moments of conversation.

"We probably shouldn't fall asleep here," Taylor reminded me when I yawned. His fingers traveled up and down my back, lulling me closer to sweet dreams. He felt so warm beneath me, an inviting pillow and absolutely, 100 percent mine.

"Fasten me up then?" I asked.

"And hide those gorgeous breasts? All of these piercings are fucking sexy."

"Play your cards right and you'll see them again soon." It took a moment, but I managed to get back into the driver's seat and turned my back to him so he could fasten my bra. "Can you handle the hooks or does your knowledge only extend to undoing them?"

"Sure." Taylor secured my bra and smoothed my

shirt down. He didn't let me go without kissing the back of my neck. "Thank you."

"Hm? What for."

"For trusting me again."

I twisted around to face him. If his excuse had been anything less, I would have walked out of his life. "I don't like lies, Taylor. You told me the truth at least, and your fibs had an actual purpose. I still don't like it, but I understand."

"If I keep anything else from you, it's because the job requires it, or I plan to tell you soon when it's safe for everyone involved, okay?"

I bit my lower lip. "Okay. I can handle that. Do you have to be at the shop tomorrow?" I asked.

"Nah. The day's all mine."

"Come home with me then," I offered.

"You're inviting me back to *your* place?"

"Of course. Now that I know I can trust you not to stash crack in my bathroom toilet or something."

I nipped his ear, and then the wind played tricks on my hearing, transforming his chuckle into a rumbling purr. The noise vibrated through the hand I'd placed over his chest.

I felt deliciously sore during the drive home, aching from our frantic union and still wet for more. I anticipated his return inside my body as I pulled into the driveway. The neighbors waved to us.

Moments later, we were inside the house with nothing but clothes between us. I bumped the door shut behind us with my hip, tossed my keys onto the hook, and threw myself into my man's arms. My weight didn't budge him. He caught me, making me feel weightless.

I spent the rest of the night learning the many ways I could get Taylor to plead for more and groan my name. The man had more energy than I'd anticipated and stamina that spoke well of his military days. He was in amazing shape.

In the pale blue, fluorescent glow of my bedside aquarium, I admired his lean physique. My fingers ran trails over his smooth chest, enjoying the muscular contours. "Are you really forty-five?"

"Yeah, why? Do I look it?" He'd sprawled on his back in my bed with one arm behind his head, the other behind my shoulders to hold me close as the sweat dried on our skin. My hair was also a mess, wild from our vigorous lovemaking and Taylor's habit of running his fingers through it while we fucked.

I walked my fingers over his flat abdomen and traced the dips between the muscles of his six pack. "Far from it."

"Good genes."

His words were an understatement. He had

amazing genes. "I wouldn't have pegged you to be any older than thirty. Though I guess I could say the same about your two friends, too."

He chuckled. "Like I said, good genes and a lot of training." His blue eyes flicked to the tank on my nightstand. "So why do you have a dozen fish tanks in your place? The bedroom, too, woman? Really?"

"I like fish," I said defensively. "It's a relaxing hobby, albeit a little expensive sometimes."

"I would have taken you for a cat person."

"Maybe… they're kind of bitchy, but recently my opinion of them has changed. You know, even though they play with their food and walk in their own poop." I thought about the cougar who sometimes came to my back door and wondered where he lived when he didn't receive food from me. Were there other humans nearby feeding him, too?

Taylor chuckled and brushed his lips across my shoulder. "Bitchy, eh? I like to think of them as having better taste than most people do."

"I'll stick with my collection of placid fish." *Unless it's my mountain lion.*

"Ouch." In a dramatic gesture, he held his hand to his heart.

"I take it you're a cat person?" *Whoops.* Giggling, I wondered if he had a pet somewhere at his other home in Houston.

"You could say that. Besides, fish swim in their poop, so..." He stuck his tongue out at me in a childish gesture.

"You're horrible."

Although he was horrible, we chatted throughout the night. I drifted off to sleep feeling warm and secure in his arms. My sexy military man would clean up Quickdraw, and in the morning, I'd certainly have more questions for him.

9

JADA

"*D*id you break up with him?" Lisa demanded when she arrived at noon the next day to set up at her station.

I froze and glanced over my shoulder at her. "Not exactly…"

She stared at me. I could read her mind, knowing her so well I thought the words before they left her mouth. "You slept with that jackass after I told you what he's doing and where you could find him dealing?"

I needed to lie. Nothing could make me give Taylor up now that I knew the truth, but ignoring Lisa wasn't an option. "I didn't make it in time, so I didn't see him dealing anything," I fibbed.

"What? You actually need to see him selling meth to believe he's doing it?"

Weed, not meth. Not that the difference matters, I thought. "I like Taylor. Not even a month ago you were threatening to go chase him yourself."

"Yeah, before I knew he was a drug-dealing creep selling shit to my kid brother."

"Your kid brother is a grown man making his own decisions, *if* what you saw was an actual drug transaction."

"Jada, dammit, I told you I snagged the drugs he bought. I can't believe you."

At the time, making love to Taylor had been easy, but the consequences of staying with him became more difficult with each passing day. In the face of Lisa's indignation, it became difficult to maintain eye contact. Standing up to my dad had been easy, but losing my friend's support hurt, leaving a deep ache in my chest.

I was the world's biggest ass.

"I really care about him, Lisa. We'll talk. I'll talk to him," I said lamely.

"Whatever."

Lisa didn't talk to me for the rest of the day. After cleaning her booth, she plucked her purse from the table and left without a goodbye. She breezed past Leigh in a huff.

"Whoa. What's her problem?" Leigh asked me, startled by Lisa's abrupt departure.

"Flip that sign to 'closed' for me and lock the door, and I'll tell you about it," I called over as I secured the register for the evening.

Leigh took a seat on the couch in the waiting area until I joined her.

"I planned to ask if you wanted to have dinner with me at The Perfect Pot, but obviously something is up. What happened?"

"Everything is a mess, Leigh. Lisa saw Taylor selling to her brother, and now she's pissed because I haven't kicked his ass to the curb."

Leigh swore. "Crap."

"Yeah. Crap."

"So that's when you called Russ?" She bit her lip and smiled faintly at my startled look. "Sorry. They called to let us know you'd found out what was going on."

"So they're all in on it?"

"Pretty much. Ian is the one who arranged for Taylor to get in the prison, so he could try to work things from the inside. He's been wanting to root out the problem, especially since they broke into our home and shot things up."

"Yeah, I remember all that from the paper. Daddy told me you had the baby home and everything."

"Yup. Dani, too. So you can understand why the guys want to get the drug issue taken care of."

I sighed and nodded. "I understand what Taylor is doing, but I don't know what to do about Lisa. Or my dad for that matter."

"Hopefully this will all be over soon. But..."

"But what?" I looked to her for advice.

"What if you two 'broke up' for the time being? Your dad would get off your case, Lisa would be appeased, and when this is all over, you two can tell everyone the truth."

"Maybe..." *Maybe that's what's best for everyone,* I thought. Leigh rubbed my shoulder in unspoken support. "I'll talk to him tomorrow, after I sleep on it."

～

TAYLOR

a police siren screamed as I crossed the bridge leading to Quickdraw. I glanced into the rearview mirror to see police lights. I pulled over clear of any potential traffic and killed the engine.

The hell is this about? I wasn't even speeding, I thought while rolling down the window. I fetched my wallet from my pocket and placed it beside me after fishing out the phony driver's license. With both set in the passenger seat, I watched the side mirror until the cop's door opened.

A lanky blond stepped from the vehicle. I made eye contact with Chief Hunt as he strode toward me, a grim expression on his face.

Fuck.

"License and proof of insurance," Hunt said in a terse voice. His hand hovered near his holster, daring me to give him a reason to fire.

"Yes, sir," I replied. I breathed in calmly and slowly reached for the glove compartment. "I'm going to get my insurance card out of here, cool?"

"That's fine."

The last thing I needed was to make him twitchy. Hunt was a good man, a great cop, but he was nervous and my record of assault put him on guard. He was within his right to be wary thanks to the impressive list of charges in Taylor Jackson's fictional history.

After the glove box fell open, I pulled the insurance card from it and placed my driver's license on top. He perused both and held on to them.

"Step out of the vehicle."

"Is something the matter, sir?" I unhooked my seatbelt.

"Step out of the vehicle," he repeated.

I didn't question it. I knew better. Wordlessly, I stepped from the car and followed him to the side of the road with both hands down to my sides, clear of my pockets.

"I have it on good authority you were seen distributing an illegal substance," he said.

Shit. Had Jada's friend ratted me out? Using my poker face, I shook my head and feigned disbelief. "I don't touch the stuff. If you don't believe me, you can search me and my car. I'm clean, sir. I give you full permission to search my person and my vehicle."

Five minutes later, another officer arrived on the scene. Hunt patted me down with his witness present then stood me alongside the road under watch while he ransacked my vehicle. When that failed, Hunt called out their canine unit to verify it was truly drug-free.

"Chief," the officer whispered, "there's nothing here. The guy is clean. You keep him here like this, everybody's going to jump to conclusions. Think it's to do with your daughter."

Every word reached my keen hearing.

Hunt shook his head and returned to task, leading the dog around again. Finally, he gave me a sheepish look when their combined efforts failed to turn up a single bud of marijuana.

"Take the dog back," he muttered to the canine handler.

"Do you want us to stay?" the other officer asked.

"No. Go on back to the station, too. I can handle it from here."

I didn't move, and neither did Hunt. We remained at the roadside in a stare off, a sort of silent, bitter stalemate until both police vehicles pulled away.

The wind kicked up, blowing grit and road dust into my face. I didn't so much as move a muscle until Hunt returned my license and insurance card to me.

"There any reason why someone would want to lie about you, son?"

I shook my head. "I try to keep to myself. If I'm not spending time with your daughter, I'm at home. I don't go out much these days."

"I've seen you at the bar with Tito's boys."

"Just once or twice. I don't really enjoy the company, if you get my drift."

Hunt watched me, skepticism in his eyes. "There anything you want to talk to me about in private, Mr. Jackson? Anything you think would help us out?"

I shook my head again. "No, sir. Nothing comes to mind."

Hunt watched me closer. "For some reason, my

daughter seems to think you're a great guy. She swears up and down you're a changed man."

"I am, sir."

"Prove it to me then. Find another job."

"There isn't another place in town for a mechanic like me to work," I pointed out.

"Go as far as Huntsville then or even Livingston. Get out of this town. Go to work in a place where you'll get some real money. A couple of the boys at the department say you worked on their vehicles and did a tip-top job. Tito's isn't the only place with openings."

"Maybe. Most people in the other towns ain't so friendly to a guy with a record," I told him. "It's not for lack of trying or being lazy. Am I free to go?"

"Yeah. You're free."

I tapped Jada's number into the speed dial as I drove away. She answered on the third ring, quicker than usual.

"Hey, baby. You busy right now?"

"Not really. What's up?" she asked.

"Your dad pulled me over as soon as I crossed the bridge. I think Lisa squealed and told him what happened."

Jada swore into the line. "Waiting for you? Seriously? *Ugh.* Yeah, she definitely told Dad. Come over to my place so we can talk, okay? No, wait. I'll meet you at yours."

I arrived to find Jada waiting for me on the porch, her car nowhere in sight. She'd walked and had taken a seat on the plastic porch chair with her hands in her lap. Jeans hugged her curves, worn with a low-cut, gold-toned blouse.

"Hey," she greeted me without getting up. "Dad didn't rough you up too bad, did he?"

"Nah, your dad is a good cop. Searched my car real good, but didn't find anything." I pulled my keys out of my pocket and unlocked the house. Jada remained in the seat after I opened the door. "You comin'?"

"About that…"

"Yeah?"

She bit her lower lip nervously and glanced away from me to the street. A car slowed down and its passenger waved to us through an open window. All of the shine was gone from her expression when she returned the friendly gesture. "I was gonna wait until tomorrow…"

"Baby, what's wrong?"

"I don't know if we should continue doing this while you have your business in town. Lisa's really upset, and I don't know if Dad really believed you."

"What are you getting at, Jada?" I lingered in the

doorway while she stood and kept her distance. "Come inside," I coaxed gently.

Reluctantly, she joined me inside after a cautious glance over one shoulder, as if certain someone was watching. Of course, in small towns, someone was *always* watching.

Once the door shut behind us, she released her inhibition and flew into my arms, squeezing me into a possessive hug. "I'm saying we should break up publically, not for real. When all of this is over, we can be open about our relationship again."

While sensible, the news still slugged me like a sucker punch to the gut. All the air left my lungs, and I deflated at the thought of going days without contact. In the little time since my lion had met her, she'd become my personal sun.

Time with Jada was the one thing I looked forward to each day of separation from friends and family. Without her, I'd have nothing.

"I understand."

"I'm not doing this because I want to, Taylor. I'm only thinking it'll be easier for you to do your job if Dad's not snooping around you because of me."

"No, you're right," I assured her. My fingers traveled up and down her back, finally reaching her ass to squeeze and knead it in my hands. "If we're going to do this, then I have a secret I need to share with you. Something important to me."

"You mean you have more than being an under-cover military spy?"

"Yeah. Something I'm trusting you with. Something only a small number of people know."

"Okay…" She eyed me up and down with caution after I released her.

I stepped back from her and pulled my shirt over my head. My belt followed.

"Uh, Taylor. I've seen all of this already." A smile touched her lips, and then her appreciative eyes roamed over my body until I kicked both jeans and boxers away. "But one more time for the road isn't a bad idea."

"I'm not stripping for sex." The cougar inside me growled, as eager to reveal itself as I was to share the secret with my chosen.

"Are you so sure about that?" she teased.

"I'm stripping because I've kept one last secret from you, and I hope after you see this, your feelings about me won't change."

I loved the sight of my boyfriend's military-trained body. As I walked my nails over his washboard abs, his stomach muscles flexed and his thick cock twitched.

"Remember, I'd never hurt you." He stepped back again until he stood beyond arm's reach.

My brows knit in confusion. "Taylor, you're freaking me out."

"I know. Just trust me, please."

Taylor's light brown skin transformed into a sandy pelt as his muscled body shrank and he fell onto all fours. Large paws replaced his strong hands, and then a long tail flicked behind him. He had a massive body for a mountain lion, with the same proud poise he carried as a man and a whiskered face with keen, familiar eyes.

Instinctively, I stumbled back against the door. My bottom hit the wood with a dull thump, but the gorgeous feline didn't move in on my personal space.

"Oh, my God," I whispered. It was the same cougar from my yard. *My* big cat. I was positive, unable to mistake the piercing blue depths gazing back at me.

A thousand questions gave way to the incredible, urgent need to touch him. I stepped forward and ran my fingers over the creature's face, touching the silky fur covering one cheek. He responded sweetly. Enormous yet docile, he was still my Taylor — the same affectionate man who held me as I fell to sleep. He purred noisily, a motor hum emanating from his chest.

"I can't believe… you've been visiting me all this time." I lowered to one knee in front of him, and a dry, pink nose touched my throat, stealing my breath away when whiskers tickled my neck.

He was human again moments later, but crouched on the floor in front of me, placing warm human flesh beneath my explorative touch. His lips skimmed from my jaw to my throat, breathing me in.

So much about him made sense.

"I mean, I knew shifters existed, but—"

"Wait, what?"

Did he expect me to go screaming out of the house? I wondered. "My cousin Suraj is a tiger shifter. They're rare in India and sort of a treasured national secret."

"I guess we both learned something new about each other." Taylor straightened and offered me both hands. One effortless tug pulled me up from the ground, but I drew free to keep my distance again.

"I need to think." Which couldn't be done while he sauntered in front of me without a stitch on his body. I gestured toward the clothing pile. Taylor caught the message and stooped to collect his duds. One glimpse at his cock was enough to make the inner muscles of my pussy flutter with need.

"Wait a minute. This means you've been following me!"

Taylor smiled sheepishly. "I meant what I said about hating you walking home at night alone. I honestly didn't realize you might think it was creepy until Russ warned me about how angry Dani was about him visiting her."

"What?"

"Dani told you about her bear, right?"

"The hammock bear, yeah."

"Well, that was Russ. All of my squad are shifters, but we have different animals," he explained.

"Dani and Leigh, too?"

"No, they're human women like you, but they accepted the guys." He inhaled a deep breath, expanding his strong ribs. "The way I hope you'll accept me."

"Is this everything? No more secrets?"

"No more secrets," he assured me. "This is me, Taylor Morrison, cougar shifter. And... I knew from the moment we met that I was meant to be yours."

"What do you mean?"

"Every shifter recognizes their true mate, Jada. We may not all find them, but we always know them when we do. You feel it, too, don't you?"

Four steps closed the distance between us and each one brought a jolt to my pounding heart. I lifted to my toes and touched my lips gently over his in a brief kiss.

"Since we've met, I can't get you off my mind. You're all I can think of. Lisa catches me daydreaming about you." I bit my lower lip, wondering how Lisa would feel once Taylor revealed his true identity to the town. "I can't stand the thought of this fake break-up, of not seeing and touching you, but it's the best thing. For both of us."

"I know," he agreed quietly, lacking the poker face I'd come to know so well. In front of me, his emotions were laid bare, exposed, and honest. "I know it's for the best, but it doesn't make me happy."

"Have…" I bit my lip. "Have you ever felt like this before?"

"No." Taylor shook his head and offered one hand. I set my palm in his and let him lead me to his small couch. "I wanted to. I tried. It was just never right. Not until you came into my life."

Our fingers twined together as we settled on the cushions. "Can I ask a question?"

"Shoot."

"Are all shifters male?"

"What gives you that idea?"

"Well, of the four shifters I know of, all are men. Is that a weird coincidence or is it a shifter thing?"

"No, we have females."

I studied Taylor's melancholy expression, surprised by the deep sadness in his eyes when I asked about female shifters.

"Did you lose someone? A mate?" I wondered out loud. The entire town knew Russ was a widower. It seemed plausible to believe Taylor could be one, too.

"Yes and no." Taylor released a heavy breath then took my other hand, holding them both between his larger palms. "Shifters can't interbreed, which means we either have to find a willing mate the same breed as us, or find love with a human. I... I was with a trio of lionesses for a while." He didn't look at me this time, focusing his attention on the double living room windows, but I caught a hint of blue peeking at me from the corner of his eye, as if judging my reaction.

"Three at once?" My voice squeaked.

"Yeah." He managed a faint smile. "Even in their human guises they prefer to live in prides. It's natural for some of us to fall into our animal habits."

The knowledge formed a lump in my stomach. "So, um, what happened? I mean, three women. Wouldn't most men kill for that?"

"As much as I cared for them, they weren't for me, Jada. Not the way you are. Fate stepped in and guaranteed we weren't compatible that way." At my confused look, he elaborated. "We couldn't have children. And for shifters, it's not something we just want. We need it. It's an innate, driven urge we all have, so we try to find mates who understand and want kids, too. When we can't procreate... or if we lose a child, it's devastating."

Taylor's voice hitched and my heart broke for him. "Is that who you lost? A child?"

He nodded in reply, jaw tense and gaze trained on the floor.

"I'm so sorry."

"We were five months along when we lost her. Not long enough to see her face, but long enough for me to know my irresponsibility caused it. It's my fault. I caused her the pain of losing a child. Most times when we meet for assignments or get-togethers, we can barely talk."

"Oh, baby, no. You can't blame yourself for something like that. I'm sure whoever she is—"

"Sasha," he said in a low, melancholy voice. "Her name is Sasha."

"I'm sure Sasha doesn't blame you either." I couldn't summon an ounce of jealousy for the woman who seemed to hold a small piece of his heart. Instead, I hurt with him, and wanted nothing more than to wash away his pain. "Do you... still miss her?"

"I miss her friendship," he said honestly. "I miss the way things were before we complicated it with a relationship. We were just friends with a physical attraction to each other, but we gambled and lost. And since she's part of the team, it makes things tense sometimes."

"So you miss hanging out with her the way we do?"

He chuckled weakly. "No. We never hung out like this. Not really. She hates video games. Couldn't drag her to a waterpark. Now one of her sisters? Isisa would come along with me for fun times, and I do miss *that*. It was like... how do I explain this? It took all three of them to come close to fulfilling me the way you do, Jada."

"Do you see them anymore? Her sisters, I mean. I feel like I have so many questions because I've never met someone in, uh, a polyamorous relationship before. It's the sort of thing you watch on a television show." I nibbled my lower lip and weakly made a joke, trying to lighten the mood. "So you had sister-wives? Is it okay to ask this stuff?"

Taylor laughed quietly, some of the warmth returning to his voice. "Yeah, it's fine. I still talk to Nandi sometimes, but... is that gonna be a problem for you?" he asked.

"There's nothing wrong with talking." I scooted into his lap and one of his arms automatically curled around my waist. "I trust you. You've hidden nothing from me that wasn't necessary."

"Thank you."

"You don't have to thank me for that, Taylor. It's the right thing to do. Do you mind answering a few more things?"

"Shoot."

"How does a relationship work with three women? Did you move from one to the next each night?"

"Nah. They had their thing before I even became involved. None of them are related, so sometimes they slept with each other. Sometimes I'd join in. It was…" He rubbed the back of his neck, a thoughtful expression on his face. "Different, I guess. I sort of felt like a fourth wheel at times. That answer your question?"

I pursed my lips thoughtfully. "Don't mountain lions usually mate and leave? How much like a mountain lion are you?"

Initially, he stared at me, then the light returned to his eyes and a crooked smile brightened his features. "I don't have any way to prove to you how much you mean to me, Jada. You'll have to take my word for it and trust me."

"Tell me more about true mates."

"All right," he agreed. "Every person in the world, human or shifter, has a soul mate. A fated mate they're meant to cross paths with at some point in their life. It may not happen when we intend for it to happen, but according to my parents, it happens when we *need* it most. Us shifters have a more acute sense of determining when it's happened. It hits us harder. We know right away, unlike humans."

His words made the decision to separate for the time being hurt even more. I peered up into his blue eyes, my brows furrowed. "And that's why you're always in my thoughts."

"Yeah. It gets a little creepy sometimes until you learn to ignore it. And of course, it's going to suck when we're apart now."

"We can still talk at night. And… now that I know you're the kitty who followed me home, maybe we can arrange something as long as you don't get yourself shot by a neighbor."

"Yeah?"

I nodded.

"I'll come tonight, if you mean it."

"Only make sure no one sees you, yeah? Most people would shoot a cougar on sight."

"I'll be careful, I promise. I was sloppy that night." The man sighed and sank back against the couch with his eyes shut, slow and rhythmic respirations moving his muscular chest. "I've been sloppy since the day I met you. My inner beast wants to claim you, and I can't fucking think when you're on my mind."

"Wait, wait, *claim* me? I'm not a mountain or a parcel of land for you to stick a flag in."

"Ha ha."

"Seriously though, what do you want to claim?"

"Shifters bond during sexual intercourse."

"We've had plenty of sex."

"Yeah, but I wasn't going to claim you without having this talk first, Jada. It's hard to explain, but it's sort of like our spirits join and become one. You have to accept it or it's worthless."

His serious tone and solemn expression gave weight to his words. As archaic as it sounded, claiming a mate obviously meant something important to him.

"So… it'll be like marrying you."

He nodded. "I know what I want, but I understand if you need time to decide. There's no rush."

"You tell me you can't get your mind off your dick when I'm around because of this, and now you tell me it's no rush?"

"Once I give myself to you, there's no taking it back, Jada. If I bond to you and for some reason you want out… you're free to leave, but you'll take part of me with you. I need to know this is what *you* want."

My eyes widened at the thought of leaving him after accepting his bond. I shook my head and opened my mouth, but my tongue had gone dry, my lips too chapped for comfort. I licked them uselessly and dropped my head. "I'll think on it," I finally uttered. "What about Leigh and Dani... have they?"

"Yeah. They did. They're your friends, so feel free to talk to them about it."

He held me for a while longer, enfolding me in his strong arms. I lost track of the time until my ringing phone jerked me back to the present.

One missed call from Daddy.

Taylor glanced at the lit screen before I put it away. "So, I guess you should storm out of here soon, huh?"

I kissed his neck instead and found the pulse point at his throat. My breath warmed his smooth jaw before I leaned in to nibble his earlobe. The act earned a small sound — one part encouragement, one part dismay. Taylor was so responsive to my touches, easy to arouse, thickening his cock from the moment my lips took their exploring path across his skin.

When I snapped open Taylor's jeans, his hard dick practically sprang up to greet me, untethered by the boxers left behind on the floor.

Mine, I thought. A sudden sense of possessiveness came over me, a desperate yearning to make him forever mine. It had to be the mating talk at work on my subconscious. Gliding my hand up and down, faster and faster, I watched his head fall back and enjoyed the rhythm of his hips, how his abs tensed and flexed, his pelvis rolled. A single, dewy drop beaded at the tip until I wiped it over the fat crown of his dick with my thumb, using the moisture to jerk him.

I felt the desire for him in my core, a longing and a soul-deep ache craving his fulfillment. I groaned out loud and released him, forcing myself to stop. A clock was unnecessary to tell the time since one glance at the darkening sky beyond the window told me night would arrive soon.

"Come once it's completely dark, and I'll finish what I started."

"Fuck," he breathed. He didn't budge from the couch.

I wanted him as much as he wanted me, wishing I could stay, strip him down, and make love to him until the sun set and our tiny town went to bed.

"I'll see you soon."

"Soon," he repeated, his breathless word a promise.

Then I stormed out of his home and onto the porch.

"And you can fucking lose my number while you're at it!" I screamed behind me, my fury displayed to an audience of three on the porch of the adjacent house.

"You okay, Jada?" his neighbor asked, a gossipy old man. Mr. Daniels liked to share other people's personal business while playing checkers at the general store. He'd share this.

"Fine," I snarled back before I stalked down the drive and out of Taylor Jackson's life.

11

TAYLOR

*W*ith a few hours to spare before nightfall, I took the opportunity for a shower and some rest. Dozing on my couch allowed me to catch up on some much needed sleep, but it wasn't the same without Russ or Nadir around to roll me off of it for catnapping.

Between Tito's new jobs for me, the time with Jada, and my own investigation, sleep had become an elusive thing I hoped to catch up with once the mission was over.

Memories of Jada's touch haunted my lucid dreaming state, and for a moment, she was there with me again, the sweet smell of her skin surrounding me with lingering traces of sandalwood and vanilla.

I wondered if she called the girls and asked them about the bonding ceremony. If they'd told her how pleasurable it was for both participants, if she was curious about how it would feel if we claimed each other as mates.

"Dispatch, be advised we have an officer down."

The report from the police band radio caught my attention, rousing me completely.

"EMS is en route to transport Chief Hunt to East Texas Medical Center."

I flew off of the couch and to my phone, hitting Ian's home line on speed dial.

"MacArthur   residence,"   Leigh   answered cheerfully.

"Evening, Leigh. Ian available right now?"

"No, but I can make him available," she chirped. The noise of the television grew fainter in the background as she moved through the house. I expected her to ask about Jada, but she didn't.

Suddenly, the thundering rush of a shower filled the phone line with noise.

"Ian! Why don't you save me some hot water and do your job. Taylor's waiting to check in," she chided. I would have chuckled at her playful tone if the circumstances weren't dire.

The water squeaked off. "It's only been fifteen minutes," Ian grumbled.

"More like thirty," she shot back. "Here you go, Taylor. Chased him out for you."

"Thanks, Leigh, you're a peach."

"She's my peach, so hands off," Ian grumbled over the line. "What's going on that you had to call me instead of Nadir?"

"Do you have the police scanner on?"

"No. Why?"

"They rushed Hunt to ETMC."

"Shit." In the background, I heard Ian scrambling around and his wife asking what was wrong. "I was in the shower, so didn't have my phone nearby. I've got a slew of text updates. They found his car overturned in the ditch. It was on fire, Taylor."

"Crap. Is he—"

"The station is calling. Hold tight and I'll call you back." Ian disconnected without further word.

For the next fifteen minutes, I paced my living room floor and tried to get ahold of Jada. She didn't answer my calls or reply to my texts. The phone rang as I was grabbing my car keys.

"Ian, man, please tell me what's going on. Jada's not picking up—"

"Jada is fine, Taylor," Ian cut in. "An officer is driving her and the rest of the family to the hospital as we speak."

Sweet relief flooded through me, tempered by

the tragedy of Chief Hunt's accident. For a moment, I'd wondered if her failure to answer my calls meant she was hurt, too.

"What happened?"

"I'm on my way to the scene. Russ is out there now and says it looks like Hunt was rammed. There's lots of glass up on the road."

"Those fuckers!" I swore.

"Taylor, it gets worse." Ian's voice had gone hard and flat, a tone I recognized from our military days. "Russ can't say for sure yet, but he's fairly certain the fire wasn't an accident. We need you to find the responsible party."

"I'm on it, man."

~

a celebratory atmosphere greeted me at the garage when I arrived around ten the next morning. Someone had splurged on name brand sodas and poured a couple dozen cans into an old cooler of ice. Lyle grilled outside by the back door. My sensitive nose picked up the juicy scent of beef burgers and beer soaked brats.

"Hell, I didn't know we were having a party. Yo, Joey, toss me a Big Red." The heavy door swung shut behind me.

"Hey, hey, T.J!" Joey greeted me with a wave and a grin. The sad fact was, he was a smart kid. Good with cars. He just made stupid decisions, and involving himself in Tito's drug operations was going to cost him.

"What's up?" I asked, accepting the frosty can of red soda he passed over.

"You hear the good news?"

"What news?" I asked, playing it safe.

"Chief Hunt is toast. Word on the street is that he was life-flighted by chopper to Houston last night, and died this morning. Ain't that fucking sweet?"

What little sympathy I had for the kid vanished in a puff of smoke. One hand tightened into a fist down at my side, the bite of nails in my palm grounding me to the moment and helping me to keep my self-control.

"Taylor. My office," Tito called me from the doorway. Drink in hand, I sauntered after the man and took the seat across from his desk.

"Something you need, Tito?"

"Only a friendly chat. Sorry about your girl-friend's Pops, but it's gotta be nice to have him out the way now, right?"

Fucking shitbag murderers. "Hell yeah, dawg. Fucker was constantly riding my ass and disre-specting me."

Am I overacting? Hell, maybe I took it too far.

Focusing on the internal script I devised in my head was the only way to diffuse my fury. The show. The performance. I had to sell my hatred of Hunt, otherwise I'd bust Tito's face open and leave his teeth on the floor.

"Besides, she dumped me yesterday afternoon after her daddy searched my car. Seems like karma got his ass, yeah?"

"Shame to hear it. That's a fine piece of woman. I'd stick my dick in that ass if I could. Anyway, that fucking pig Hunt wasn't the only distraction around here. MacArthur's poking his nose into the shit already."

The thought of Tito putting his slimy hands anywhere near Jada made my skin crawl. I dragged a deep breath into my lungs and tried to appear aloof. "I hear he's a legend around here."

"A legendary asshole," Tito spat. "If we didn't have him around, we'd be set, but getting that man is impossible."

"Sounds like you've tried." *Admit it, you piece of shit.*

"A few of the boys may have been party to an attempt on the man's life. That mess cost me the last police chief. The boss man wasn't pleased."

I whistled, feigning awe as part of the performance. "Shiiiit, too bad you don't have another chief in your pocket along with Judge Fitz. How's it working out with him now anyway?"

"Whatever you did worked."

"Heh. You need to know where to apply the pressure, is all."

Tito grunted. "If only MacArthur was so easy."

"Why isn't he easy? The man isn't bullet proof, right?"

"He isn't. Getting to him is the hard part. It's like he has a sixth sense for this thing. He's never around in an easy place."

"What about a hit at his place?" I asked. My stomach knotted with tension as I faced the internal dilemma of advising Tito on how to take out my best friend.

"Tried that," Tito replied. "Now he's on to us and it's impossible."

Almost a year ago, a bunch of thugs had driven up to Ian's house and kicked in the door. They'd failed to kill him because Russ and Ian were out conducting an investigation in their animal forms.

Since then, he'd had gates, a twelve foot fence, and cameras installed to surround his hundreds of acres.

"So, what's stopping you guys from doing it when he's in town?" I asked.

"Like I said, he seems to have a sense for this thing. I called you in here for a specific purpose. Lyle says your sort are attracted to the same area like bees to honey. Where one shifter goes, a dozen more will follow. I need someone capable of taking out MacArthur, and the boss is willing to pay fifty thousand dollars to see it happen."

It could be the opportunity to blow the case wide open. Who was the damned big boss pulling the strings around Quickdraw and why was Ian's death worth so much to him? "What if I kill him?" I offered slowly. "Nobody has a reason to suspect me. Hunt maybe, but one of your guys took care of him, right? Let me handle this one."

"This ain't the same as putting the fear of God into an old man. He's a shifter like you, remember?"

"I've killed before." I had. "It's no big deal." It was. Maybe I'd killed in the service of my country, but I'd never enjoyed it.

"Good. The boss wants it done sooner than later. Get this done, T.J., and maybe you'll be meeting him in person to receive your payment." Tito slid a gun across the desk to me.

I had no choice but to accept it.

"Nadir, get the team together. They want Ian dead next."

"What?" By his slurred voice, it sounded as if I'd woken Nadir out of a sound sleep. He rarely kept normal hours.

"Tito's giving me a chance to prove myself and get rid of an obstacle. I need you and Juni to prep Ian for a hit."

"Another attack at his place?" Alarm raised the volume of Nadir's voice. "What the hell did you agree to?"

"No. Nothing like that," I assured him, pulling a beer from the fridge. "Ian's got to die, and it's gotta be soon, man. I told Tito I'd give this my personal touch to get him out of the way. I don't want Leigh or Sophia involved at all."

"Fuck. Okay, yeah. Lemme get in touch with him and see what we can do." Drawers opened and closed in the background, followed by the sound of rustling clothes. "Did you have something in mind?"

"It needs to be public. Something fast, so Tito's thugs don't have time to go and check the body, but with no chance of hitting bystanders."

"Give us a day to get something together—"

I cut him off, voice sharp. "I don't have a day."

"Are you kidding me? Stall it out and tell Tito

you're working on a plan. Tell him you're gonna case Ian some, get his daily routine down 'cause you don't want to land your ass back in prison."

"I don't know about that. They're expecting me to produce results."

"Taylor, look, man, I know you're upset, but if we rush this, there's a good chance Ian will *actually* die. None of us want that. As for Tito, he wants you to get this done. Not botch it up in hate."

"Fine," I relented. "Three days, no more. Soon as you guys concoct something, I want to know."

"Of course. Have you talked with Jada? We got the news today about her father," Nadir said.

"No. Her shop is dark, and her car isn't in her drive."

"She's staying with her mom and brother. My folks took some casseroles over yesterday evening."

The knowledge only partially relieved my anxiety. "I've tried calling."

"Get over there and see her, man. She could really use you right now."

"I'm pretty sure if I knock on her mom's door, I'll be getting arrested."

Nadir sighed and I easily pictured him shaking his head at whatever dumb thing I'd said. "Go do what cats do best, Taylor. Paw at a window or something."

I took his advice.

Ninety minutes later, under the cover of darkness, I prowled through the bushes surrounding the Hunt household. They lived in a ranch style house on a large lot with several oak trees in the yard. Avoiding the lights, I peeked through the windows one at a time until I found Jada. She lay sprawled on her stomach across a twin-sized bed covered with tropical fish themed blankets. After turning a page in the book in front of her, she wiped her tear-streaked face with a tissue.

Certain she was alone in the dimly lit room, I batted at the window with my paw. Jada startled at the sound and glanced to the window. Surprise widened her red-rimmed eyes, but she hurried over without fear and opened the window and sliding screen.

"Taylor?" she whispered.

I answered by nuzzling her face then leapt inside after she moved aside. My transformation back into my human skin was instant and effortless, and then Jada was in my arms.

"I'm here, baby," I crooned against her hair. "I'm here."

"He's dead," she blubbered. Hot tears leaked against my naked skin. "Daddy's dead."

Guiding her to the bed, I snagged a blanket to

drape over my lap then pulled her down against me. The book she'd tossed aside turned out to be an old photo album. Chief Hunt beamed up at me from a picture on the opened page. A younger Jada was pictured with him in front of a sandy beach on the shoreline.

I held her for as long as she needed, letting the minutes pass while my hand smoothed up and down Jada's back. She didn't speak until her sobs subsided.

"Thank you, Taylor... for coming," she added in a thick voice. Another shudder ran through her. Then she muffled the next sob against my chest. "I can't believe Dad's gone."

"He was a great man, and the world's a poorer place without him in it. I only wish I'd gotten the chance to know him as the real me."

"He'd have loved you," Jada whispered, sniffling.

"Is this your old room?"

"Yeah. Mom's kept it as is, though she keeps threatening to turn it into a sewing room."

Looking around was like peeking into Jada's past. Old pom-poms hung on the wall beside a framed school certificate and blue ribbon for the science fair. A colorful fish poster hung over the twin-sized bed.

"Taylor?"

"Yeah?"

"Can you stay tonight?"

"What if your mom peeks in?" The last thing I wanted was to upset her mom after she lost her husband.

"She won't. One thing Mom and Dad were always good about was respecting our privacy. As much as she may try to meddle sometimes, my room is like... sacred ground."

"Okay." I kissed her brow, decision made. "But I'll have to sneak out before dawn. Easier to slink through town when it's dark."

"Deal."

We crawled under the blanket and cuddled close on the narrow bed. The somber circumstances kept potentially lustful thoughts at bay. My cougar's perpetual need for Jada diminished in favor of providing her comfort.

"I promise, Jada, I'm going to get whoever killed your dad," I vowed.

"How?" she asked in a tiny voice.

"Best you not know the details. Just know that I'm not going to let them get away with this. Until then, you stay away from Tito's, okay?"

"Did he do it?"

"Nah, he doesn't have the guts. This came from above him, and that's who I'm after. I take down their boss and I get them all."

The beast inside of me demanded a chance to soothe her. I relinquished my control and shifted in the bed, exchanging human flesh for fur, hands for paws. Without a word, Jada snuggled into me and closed her eyes. Our embrace became as natural as breathing, no different in my feline form as it had been as a man.

"Your whiskers tickle," she whispered.

I responded with a purr, rumbling the noise and tucking my head beneath her chin. Jada stroked her fingers down my back. She made the tiniest sound, as consoled by my presence as any woman could be on the night after losing her father.

Exhaustion gradually claimed her, but before it took hold, she kissed my nose in unspoken appreciation. I remained beside my future mate until her breaths evened out and slumber relaxed her body. Then I stayed a little longer, breathing in her scent and loathing the necessity of my eventual departure. Before the sun rose, I snuck from the bed and let myself out through the unlocked window.

I wouldn't let Jada down. Someone had to be held accountable for her dad's death, and I was determined to find the person behind it.

12

TAYLOR

"You ready for this?"

The driver, a husky Hispanic guy called Paco, twisted around in his seat to look at me. I sat in the rear of a white Volkswagen van, clothed in my dark sweats. My black and white bandanna was loosely tied around my neck, ready to be raised around my face.

"Yeah. Coast is clear, right?"

"Ain't a cop around here," Joey said. "Don't forget your shades, dude. You the only black dude around here with eyes like that."

"Sorta circumstantial," Paco muttered. "They can't pinch him over eye color and race."

"Nah, he's right. They can try and make shit hard for me."

Going into a hot zone never gave me the nervous jitters. I felt at home when on a mission, but this was different. This was my friend. My comrade. I had to pretend to shoot Ian down in cold blood, and I wasn't using blanks. One wrong shot would be enough to turn our charade into reality.

I took in a few deep breaths and hopped out of the van. A dark alley stretched between the post office and pharmacy, a place often traveled by pedestrians traveling on foot to pick up mail from their post office boxes.

The Quickdraw Post Office didn't deliver to in-town residents, so Ian picked up his grandmother's newspaper, bills, and correspondence each day if Leigh didn't fetch it herself.

I hung beside the trimmed hedge and watched Ian emerge from the quiet building. The sound of my own pulse thundered in my ears, deafening against the tranquil evening.

Ian walked down the post office steps, a handful of envelopes in his hand. *Now or never.* I leapt out with the gun raised, lined up my shot down the sights, and squeezed the trigger. Ian jerked back and stumbled from the impact. Blood splattered over the front page of the Quickdraw Chronicle. Then the handgun barked and jumped in my hand, releasing another bullet.

A woman across the road locked up the doors to her gift shop. Shrieking, she leapt into her car for cover. She had to be calling 9-1-1 by now, if the shots fired weren't enough to bring the police.

The final shots were a blur. I ran my ass off down the alley and leapt into the van waiting for me at the other end. Paco peeled off down the road and hauled ass around the corner into the Dixie Quarters where cops rarely traveled. Back there, it was lawless squalor and one-bedroom shacks housing meth labs. Back there, social workers made frequent visits to remove children from neglectful homes.

Fuck, fuck, fuck. I pulled the bandana off and tossed it onto the floor.

"He dead?"

"He wasn't moving when I left."

Please don't be dead. Please.

"Whoo boy! MacArthur riddled with holes." Joey pumped his fist in the air.

"Pull in there, Paco. The shit-green house with the open garage. We'll spray paint this ride up in no time," Joey said.

Lyle met us in the house after we pulled the van in and shut the rust-spotted door. Empty beer cans littered his kitchen counters and the whole place reeked of wet dog. The disgusting odor turned my stomach.

"How many shots did he take, T.J?" Lyle asked.

"I damn near emptied the mag in his sorry ass. He never saw me comin'."

"Tito wants you to come by the old station first thing in the morning. By that time, we should know if you killed the bastard or not. Until then, we paint the van and lay low."

I pulled off my black sweatshirt and tossed it onto the grill to be burned. The bandanna followed, then Joey squirted a liberal amount of lighter fluid over it before tossing in a match.

"You guys can lay low, but I'm heading back into town this evening. It'll be suspicious if I disappear."

"I don't know about that," Lyle interrupted, ever the loyal dog to his master.

"Yeah, well, let's see you stop me. I did the job, and now I'm gonna head home to chill." I still hadn't figured out his breed, but I imagined it was something small and spineless. A beagle maybe.

To my surprise, Lyle stepped up to me and blocked the way. "I know you think you're hot shit, but Tito put me in charge—"

I rose up to my full height and hissed at him. Lyle shrank back a step, quickly put off by the hint of my cougar I allowed him to see.

"What was that about?" I heard Joey asking as I moved outside into the sunlight.

I took a dusty, dirt path as a shortcut, avoiding the main streets. No one gave me a second glance in passing. The moment I stepped inside, I flipped on the television to the local news. A reporter stood outside the Post Office, yellow tape stretched across the narrow street behind her.

"Sheriff Ian MacArthur was pronounced dead on scene. Police are on the lookout for an adult male suspect. Witnesses at the scene described an African American male, approximately six feet tall."

The reporter rattled off a vague description fitting at least a quarter of Quickdraw's residents. I shook my head.

Hours passed before Nadir's call came through on one of our untraceable, private lines.

"Everything's okay. We've got Ian with us at the bunker. He's going to lay low here for a while until it's time for him to resurface."

We kept a place for special circumstances. The bunker, located deep in the middle of nowhere, housed our goods, weapons, and computer equipment. It was a control center for our missions and a place where Juni, our communications expert, created new gadgets for us to use in security jobs local to Texas.

"Thank God."

"He's impressed by your shooting, you should

know. He says the shot to the thigh hurt like a son of a bitch, but he's already up and walking around. Sasha had it stitched in minutes. It looked real. Better than we could have hoped for."

"Yeah, well, he was a good teacher."

He and Russ both. Sagging back against the couch, I closed my eyes and wondered what Jada was doing. I'd promised to bring her father's murderers to justice, and I had to see this through to the end.

"Now what's going on with our shitheads?" my squad mate asked.

I told Nadir everything, and by the end, I could laugh with him since the stone-cold weight in my chest had dissipated.

"You think this will get you to the boss?"

"They want me down at the old train station in the morning."

"Get some rest then."

"What about Leigh and Betty?"

"They know what's up. Ian explained it all to his grandmother yesterday and sent her to visit an old friend out of state. She's gambling on some riverboat casino as we speak."

"Lucky."

"Agreed. Leigh and Sophia are with Dani and Russ, playing the part of the grieving widow. He told her last night to prepare her for it."

"So what's the plan?"

"Hang on a sec. Ian wants to talk to you. He has an idea."

"Hey, Taylor. I have some thoughts about your meeting tomorrow. We don't know where they plan to take you, so I'd like you to wear one of Juni's GPS gadgets," Ian said.

"I'll sew that little button mic on my shirt since she's so proud of creating it."

"Good. What I also propose is that I come in my eagle form now, perch near your place, and follow you in the morning."

"Sounds good," I agreed.

We made plans for Ian to follow by air with one of Juni's tiny transmitters around his leg. The rest of the team would monitor my location and follow at a discreet distance, ready to act once Ian gave the signal.

Sleep was hard to come by, but somehow I managed a few restless hours. I woke up early and headed out, comforted by the sight of Ian circling overhead. An old beat up truck that may have been red at some point was parked by the abandoned building when I arrived. Tito waved me over through the window and told me to climb in.

"Where we going, boss?"

"You'll see."

A thirty-minute drive into the boonies brought us to our destination. The building resembled an old barn from the outside. Rotted wood planks and rusted barbed wire disguised the true operation.

Tito led me inside. The exterior was busted, but the barn had been gutted and given an appropriate makeover to house what may have been one of the largest drug manufacturing centers in East Texas. Workers in their underwear — stripped to remove any doubt of stealing the precious product — packaged drugs for distribution onto the streets. Their mules had to be carrying coke and meth as far as Houston. No. Maybe even Dallas.

His employees appeared to be all ages, genders, and ethnicities without discrimination. Anybody could cut cocaine and dry hash for Tito's small-time dealers to sell.

We passed a hydroponic growing room with rows of marijuana plants beneath hanging UV lamps along with some thugs with guns and cocky expressions who didn't bother to ask if I was strapped, too.

As we passed, a whisper reached me from one of the boys. "Yo, I heard he's the one who iced MacArthur."

We stopped in front of a closed door. Tito shot me a look. "Mind your manners with the boss, T.J.

Don't embarrass me. You play your cards right in here and you'll be going places in this business."

"No worries, Tito. It's cool."

Tito pushed open the heavy metal door and gestured me in ahead of him. Much like his space at the garage, the office was decked out in an opulence that contrasted with the sparse squalor outside. Buck heads were mounted on the walls, but I gave them little more than a passing glance. Instead, my gaze focused on the man dominating the room.

The guy was bigger than Russ with trapezius muscles so huge he barely had a neck above his shoulders. His pale, bald head gleamed beneath the sunlight pouring through the old barn window. Deep down, part of me was glad the brains behind the entire operation wasn't a member of the Mexican drug cartels.

That would have complicated matters greatly.

"So, you're Taylor. I heard we got reason to celebrate because of you, kid."

"Yes, sir."

"Polite." The boss smirked then looked me up and down, sizing me up. "Call me Beau. Sir is so... formal. You and I are gonna be working too close for that."

"Good to meet you, Beau. I didn't do much, though."

"Ha! You hear that, Tito? 'Not much' he says." Beau chortled and crossed over to his desk. "No more of MacArthur poking his big fucking nose into my business. He's a difficult man to get to, but you caught him at a particularly vulnerable time. I respect that."

"I believe in getting the job done. I've made more money working for Tito than I ever earned on my own selling pot."

"That so?" Beau looked me over again.

"I got no reason to lie. You guys have a nice operation going."

"I started over in New Orleans, built my business up from the ground. I've got runs from Mexico into the bayou as well as this backwater dump," Beau boasted. "Once, I was like you, Taylor. Just a low man on the totem pole."

"And now you're the big boss."

The man chuckled and pointed his finger at me. "Exactly so, Taylor. I did what needed to be done, exactly as you're doing now. Which leads me to a question for you."

"Shoot."

"You ready to take over a part of this business?"

"Hell yeah. Why me though?"

"You did what nobody else around here had the balls to do. Thought I'd have to come personally to take out MacArthur myself after my boys botched the last attempt. But I didn't. You took some real initiative, offered to get rid of a problem Tito couldn't squash. He says you ain't a half-bad thief either, that y'all successfully knocked over McMillan Pharmacy with a plan you created."

"Don't wanna toot my own horn or anything, but yeah, I'm good at setting shit up."

A draft from one of the air vents blew a peculiar scent to me. Something about Beau was familiar, tickling my senses.

It's... I've smelled this before. The dry, almost spicy scent taunted me with its familiarity. The earthen muskiness brought to mind some of the reptiles I'd hunted while in the wilderness with Nadir.

He's a fucking shifter like us. Suddenly, Tito's unusual knowledge of our world made sense. He knew more beyond Lyle, because the big, all-powerful boss overseeing their criminal career was one, too.

"What kind of cat are you?" Beau asked, cutting to the chase.

"I'm a cougar," I answered promptly without missing a beat.

"Walk with me."

Beau led the way back through the warehouse, Tito trailing behind us several feet. From the corner of my eye, I spotted Lyle among the guards watching the workers.

"I don't have any need for another human on payroll," Beau said in a low voice, chuckling. "They're a dime a dozen, but men like you are rare in this business."

"Tito seems to do all right."

We stepped into the clearing outside the barn. Beau turned to me with a gun in hand. I hadn't even seen him pull it out. For a heart stopping moment, I thought he knew the truth. My pulse roared in my ears and my muscles tensed.

Ian watched from nearby in the branches of a tree overlooking the barn. His trilling call carried through the air, a warning that help was near. I counted the number of warbles, five in all meant five minutes stood between me and assistance. I saw him lean forward and partially open his wings, prepared to take flight and come to my aid. Like me, he waited to see what happened.

Beau flipped the gun in his hand and offered it to me, butt first.

"What's this?" I asked, accepting the weapon.

"The task is simple. You want the promotion, shoot Tito and take his place."

Damnit, I need Tito. Death is too good for him. Beau

left me with few choices. Without further hesitation, I turned on Tito with the gun raised.

"What the fu—?"

The sharp retort of the 9mm filled the air, followed by Tito's pained yell. Red blossomed against his obnoxious yellow pants then he collapsed to the ground, gripping his bleeding thigh.

Lyle moved quickly to his master's side and growled, protective and loyal to the end. Too bad I couldn't shoot him, too.

"Like to have some fun with your kills, eh? Guess that's typical of cats. Don't worry, Lyle, you'll have a new master."

"You said shoot him. Not kill," I said when I came under the scrutiny of Beau's beady eyes.

"Rather keep him on as help. I get it." Beau nodded his head, impressed. "Pragmatic. Besides, I suppose he'll have some use. Tito's been in contact with some flesh dealers down in Houston. Working on some mergers."

The news turned my stomach. Swallowing down the bile rising in my throat, I maintained a neutral expression and answered with a terse nod. "I didn't know you guys were into selling hos, too. Is that moving to Quickdraw by any chance?"

"Yeah. You ain't soft about keeping a few girls in line are you?"

I shook my head. "Not really. Where are they coming from? Europe?"

"Some. We get a few from Latin America, too. Guatemala and Venezuela. You promise girls a better life in America and they're eager to come."

Girls. In my head I imagined scared and terrified teenagers who didn't know any better, fleeing from poverty and starvation in hopes of a better life.

It became more difficult to keep my cool.

"So what does this have to do with me?"

"You, my friend, will be taking over the business in Quickdraw. I need a man with some presence and power behind him to keep these fools in line."

Lyle hadn't moved from above Tito. From the corner of my eye, I saw the man watching me, his posture low and protective, as if he'd leap onto Tito and take a bullet if I changed my mind.

Maybe he would. Dogs were loyal, even if their masters were shit.

I turned the weapon on Beau instead. "Keep your hands where I can see them."

The amusement faded from his face and his black eyes hardened. "You're funny, kid. Now hand over the gun."

"I'd rather drag your sorry ass to jail," I spat out.

Beau didn't appear surprised by the revelation. "So, Tito brought me a mole." The big boss nodded to the two men by the door. "Kill him. Kill them both."

They raised their guns, but my reflexes were faster. I shot both as Beau exploded out of his suit. A massive, thirteen-foot-long crocodile was left behind, and it advanced on me with a burst of speed. Pulling the trigger while stumbling back from him meant most of my shots flew wide. Three sank into the croc's meaty, powerful body, but the rest hit the dirt at his sides.

Fuck me! I'd been guessing at a snake, not a muscled monster full of sharp teeth.

I managed to get enough space between us to rip out of my shirt and shift, but my pants hindered my escape, tangling around my hind legs. While I struggled to get out of my clothes, the enemy advanced.

Lyle leapt forward, transitioning from man to dog in midair. He kicked out of his jeans and wriggled from his shirt. I twisted and leapt to the side to avoid allowing him to come up on my rear. Batting with one claw kept him at bay, or so I thought, until the big, red-colored coonhound landed on Beau to attack him instead.

Tito may have treated him like shit, but Lyle loves him, I realized. *Loves him enough to be loyal and fight for both of their lives.*

Lyle growled and snapped his teeth in a failed

attempt to get ahold of the crocodile. Beau knocked him off and slammed the dog aside with his strong tail. Then he turned on me.

If the crocodile got ahold of any part of me, the fight would end. He'd roll me, rip me to pieces, and I'd be dead before help arrived.

Light on my feet, I ducked and moved to the side, prancing out of his way. He snapped and twisted his body with his jaws open, seeking my foreleg. I landed safely to his left and tried to close my teeth around the back of his head. He jerked too quickly for me and I missed.

Damnit!

Our fight attracted attention from the guards inside. Three men rushed out with the guns raised and tried to make out the situation. As far as they were concerned, there was only one enemy. Me.

"Shoot 'em, man!" one of the guards cried out. Lucky for me, they were crap shots. Bullets struck the ground and spit up dirt. One grazed my left shoulder and drew a stinging line of blood.

Several vehicles rumbled into view down the dirt road, kicking up clouds of dust. They stomped their brakes then doors flew open as law enforcement officers flooded out. Texas Rangers. They'd arrived at last.

Among them, I saw our squad mates.

Sasha was leaned out a window with a rifle against her shoulder. One well-aimed shot took down a guard and drove the other two toward cover. It became a full on shoot-out between my back-up and the complex guards. Two more men ran out from the building and opened fire on the Rangers.

Ian dove down from the skies and raked his sharp talons at Beau's beady face, aiming at the eyes. The crocodile snapped at him. A single brown feather drifted to the ground as Ian soared upward out of range. Outnumbered, but not defeated, Beau turned toward the weakest of us within his reach.

Tito.

The wounded man pushed up onto his hands and made a frantic effort to escape. Beau charged after him. Before he reached his target, the coonhound raced in and placed himself between Tito and our common enemy.

Beau's massive jaws closed around the dog's leg. Then the croc performed the devastating attack I'd feared. Lyle yelped and screamed in pain as Beau rolled across the dusty ground. Blood splattered the dirt, and then the dog was free — bleeding, missing his left foreleg, but free. The coppery, metallic scent filled my nostrils.

Lyle and Tito were dirtbags, but I couldn't stand by as Beau devoured them. I darted in. My speed allowed me to keep out of Beau's biting range, but his strong attacks kept me from moving in close enough for a lethal blow.

Nadir charged in and squeezed off a round. He missed the brain, but the shock of a bullet wound drew Beau's attention off me. That split second was all I needed.

My jaws closed around the back of his neck, and he thrashed, putting up a futile struggle that ended when my teeth severed his spine. The gator went limp.

Ian's friends in the Texas Rangers knew about our special gifts. The Ranger in the lead, a balding man in his early forties, rushed forward with his gun drawn. I heard him shouting, "The puma is one of us!"

I shifted to my human form, and with the back of my wrist, wiped Beau's blood from my mouth. The Rangers stared. Two of the guys — I recognized their faces from another bust — had seen us make transitions before. For some humans, it probably never got old.

Juni tossed me a bag with clothes. I dressed while the authorities handled the workers inside. Sasha applied a tourniquet to Lyle's spurting stump while Nadir handcuffed Tito. If not for her quick intervention, the hound shifter would have died on the dusty pavement and bled out.

"Call for medical. This one needs emergency care," Sasha called to Nadir. She'd crouched beside Lyle to hold his remaining hand. Always kind and compassionate, she wouldn't abandon him to lie afraid and hurting. "I'm going to give you a dose of morphine, okay?" she said to him.

"Please, anything. It hurts so bad," Lyle moaned.

I loved her still, but it was a different kind of love. The love for a close friend and comrade had eclipsed any former physical attraction. Jada was the one who had captivated my heart.

Ian emerged from the trees dressed in jeans and a t-shirt. He joined up with the lead Ranger and shook his hand.

"It's going to take days to process the mountain of evidence here, on top of what your man has retrieved." The Ranger nudged his cowboy hat up his forehead.

"I told you he'd get the job done. You all right, Taylor?" Ian called over.

"You owe me a shit ton of paid leave after this."

"Deal."

~

*J*an made a dramatic return from the dead, stunning most of the town.

Thankfully, neither Lyle nor Tito died from their injuries. The dog survived, barely, and in appreciation of his help at the end, I managed to convince them to cut him a plea bargain so he'd stand trial and testify in our favor.

He and Tito told everything about the operation and even ratted out a trio of Texas politicians in on the entire thing.

The next day, arrests swept over East Texas as warrants were issued naming powerful men and women. A half dozen judges, several politicians, and even corrupt law enforcement officers lost their good reputation when the hammer came down. A few corrupt prison bosses were swept into the scandal. Tito named two captains, a major, and a couple wardens across the state.

The family of Dennis James would finally receive justice for his murder.

When asked about Chief Hunt's death, Lyle clammed up and Tito claimed he hadn't ordered the hit.

"He says he won't talk to anyone but you about it. We need you in the room if they're going to get his confession," Ian told me.

"Okay. That's cool," I agreed.

While Tito's flesh wound had already received treatment, requiring his release to the jail, the same wasn't true for his dog. I arrived to the hospital and rode the elevator to the second floor where law enforcement officers waited outside the man's room. He lay in the bed, pathetic and pale, his carrot-colored hair bright against his pale, waxy cheeks. Ankle cuffs secured his feet and a restraint belt restricted movement of his remaining arm.

It wasn't like the cop shows made it out to be. No two-way mirror, no lawyers in suits. I nodded to the Ranger and officer standing watch over the confession; then I pulled up a seat beside the bed.

"Hey, Lyle. You look like hell."

"Whatever, pussy."

I let the halfhearted insult roll off me. "I hear you won't talk to them about Hunt. Why me?"

"Why'd you tell 'em to cut me a plea bargain?" he asked in return. "You hate me."

"Hate's a strong word. Besides, you saved my life."

"Wasn't trying to save you," he said, brown eyes boring into me.

"I know. End result is still the same though, ain't it? They told me you won't talk unless I'm here."

"Why'd you stop Beau from killing me and Tito?

You coulda got enough shit to make your case without us."

"It was the right thing to do. A wise man once said, 'The only thing necessary for the triumph of evil, is that good men do nothing.' Maybe that makes me a pussy in your eyes, but my conscience is clear."

"All right. Tell that nurse to bring my shot of morphine, and I'll talk."

"Talk first. I won't have you drugged up and high. I wanna know about Chief Hunt. Was it you? Is that why you won't fess up?"

Lyle shook his head. "Wasn't me."

"Then who? Cooperating will go a long way in helping your case."

"Joey killed Hunt. He took one of our trucks and ran him down in his police cruiser. Said he wanted to impress Tito the way you always did whenever you was around. Said he wanted more responsibility."

"And the fire?" I asked.

"The kid started it when the gas tank began to leak. He told me he didn't wait around to see if Hunt was already dead, so he torched the shit to be on the safe side before he drove off."

"How do we know you aren't making this up?"

"Tell Tito I talked. Ain't like we got a way to communicate in here."

With some pressure, Tito confirmed Lyle's report of the events. The police arrested Joey an hour later for murder, fulfilling my promise to Jada to find her father's killer.

My work in Quickdraw was finished, but my life there had only begun.

EPILOGUE

DECEMBER

JADA

I stole a glance at Taylor from where I stood on the brides' side of the aisle. No man had ever looked finer in a military uniform than mine, but the two grooms were a definite close second. The love shining from Russ and Ian's faces was enough to make anyone smile.

The four men standing at the front were undeniably sexy, Nadir and Taylor both serving as groomsmen, while I, Dani's little sister Marta, and a few of her cousins stood in as bridesmaids.

The two brides, stunning visions in similar dresses, put the rest of us to shame, their beauty beyond comparison to the rest of us.

Daniela and Leigh walked down the aisle together, arm in arm. They wore strapless gowns, but the similarity ended there. Dani wore her waist length tresses in an exquisite updo, while Leigh's hung around her shoulders in loose spirals. As the taller of the two women, Leigh chose flats, but Dani wore heels. The fair-skinned blonde resembled a princess in her pale pink, ruffled, taffeta dress. Our Latina friend was equally beautiful in her airy, chiffon layers of pale ivory.

Lisa, Naomi, and I did a damned good job putting the two women together. I beamed with pride, sniffled, and dabbed my cheeks again with a handkerchief, moved by the brides' radiant expressions. Most of the town had shown up for the double ceremony and packed every pew in the church.

The same church where Leigh and Ian first met.

My mother had loaned both brides her own bridal jewelry. Something blue to honor the wedding traditions. Dani wore a thick gold necklace with large sapphires. The dangling gold segments fell in chandelier style, tapering to a V pointed toward Dani's corset-enhanced cleavage. Leigh had the matching tiara tucked against her blonde curls. Participating in the wedding preparations had given Mom something to do and occupied her mind from Dad's death.

I thought it would be too rough on her at first, but I was wrong, and for the first time in nearly two months, she was smiling again. Her eyes were bright.

I loved my mother. No matter how much we argued during my childhood, she'd always been Mom, looking out for me and trying to do what was best. The tears I'd struggled so hard to keep at bay spilled over my cheeks. I'd probably look a hot mess by the time the photographer came around to snap pictures of the bridal party again.

The joint ceremony was simple with each couple exchanging personal vows. We blew bubbles and tossed rose petals on them as they left the church. Some of the younger guests had tied a row of tin cans to the rear bumper of Russ and Ian's vehicles.

Taylor and I rode in his Cadillac to the wedding reception. Ian had rented Lottie's for all of their close friends and family to enjoy a private dinner. Soft music played over the speakers and two stunning tiered cakes were displayed in the center of the room. A single chocolate and strawberry groom's cake sat between them, the one flavor Russ and Ian could agree to share.

I ended up chatting with the two brides while Taylor moved away to mingle with his squad and their mutual friends. A tap to the shoulder pulled me from conversation about their honeymoon travel plans. I'd offered to watch Sophia for Leigh and Ian, thrilled to have a toddler to spoil. Taylor promised to help.

"Jada?"

"Hm?" I answered as I turned. I came face to face with Taylor and an angelic blonde. "This is Sasha. She wanted to meet you."

Sasha was my complete opposite; tall, lithe, and golden with white-blonde hair tamed into a chic updo. Picturing her as a proud lioness was easy. Without further introduction, the woman leaned in and embraced me, squeezing me with warm affection.

"You've got a good man here," she said. "I'm really happy for both of you." She had a peculiar accent I couldn't place.

"Thanks, Sasha," I replied as she ended the hug. I bit my lip and searched the restaurant for two equally hot blondes. "Are the other two with you?"

Sasha blinked her blue eyes in surprise, glancing from me to Taylor then back again. "They are, but we didn't all want to swarm and smother you."

"I'd love to meet them. Taylor has nothing but good things to say." I understood his relationship with the trio and felt no reservations.

He was mine, and nothing would change that.

Nandi and Isisa weren't what I expected. They

had skin like dark mahogany, smooth and flawless. Their contrasting figures, one plump and curvy like me, the other muscular and toned, appeared beautiful in gold dresses. The shade was a perfect match to their almond-shaped eyes. Both greeted me with smiles, although only Isisa leaned in for a hug as Sasha had.

"I am happy for you. For both of you," Isisa said.

African. They're definitely from Africa, I thought. It made sense in a strange sort of way, considering their animal form.

"Thank you. It's great to finally meet."

Maybe another woman would feel awkward or even intimidated by the meeting, but I didn't, not when their open and genuine expressions held so much happiness for us.

So I told them about my new shop and learned Isisa was a lawyer with a practice in Houston. Their pride sister, Nandi, dabbled in self-publishing, a quiet introvert who often kept to herself.

"Any time you girls want to come down to Quickdraw for a day to relax, let me know." I took a card out of my small clutch purse and scribbled my cell phone number on the back. Sasha accepted it as if I'd handed her a precious gem instead. Her wide blue eyes filled with surprise.

We hugged again — Nandi, the shyest lioness,

even squeezed me briefly — then the three breath-taking women moved on.

Taylor and I slipped out shortly after the brides and their grooms. Only a couple months ago, he'd begun construction on a new home in the Quick-draw outskirts where Ian and Russ lived. While I had given plenty of advice during the building stages, I hadn't yet had a look at the finished product.

And I couldn't wait to see.

~

TAYLOR

"So, what do you think?" I asked when we reached the empty living room. We had rounded back through another set of doors from the kitchen into a vast space with a row of big windows displaying the monstrous front yard.

"My opinion is the same, hon. You definitely have a lot to grow into," Jada commented, referring to the tour of my new, but empty, two story brick house. I'd built it between Russ and Ian's homes. "That's a big-ass yard. Who's gonna take care of all of that?"

A fifty-yard driveway snaked through the trees and a sprawling pasture to reach my place. Ian had given me my pick of the lots he owned, so I chose a place with room to roam.

"Russ will. They have a tractor over at their place."

In a week, I planned to bring most of my belongings from Houston. The four-car garage provided the space for both of my vehicles and room for Jada's car, if I could convince her to take the next step in our relationship. The rest of the place was a modest, brick exterior with wood floors and a woman's dream kitchen.

Jada never claimed a love for cooking, but she'd bitched about my tiny kitchen in the old place I'd rented. Prepared to house her immense wardrobe, I'd also given the architect specific instructions for an enormous walk-in closet with a built-in shoe rack.

Nobody owned more footwear than my girl.

"I haven't exactly had the time to shop for furniture," I muttered.

"You did this to yourself when you decided to buy and takeover Tito's business." She leaned up to kiss me, barely touching our lips.

Jada undid the buttons on my dress uniform jacket, but not before she skimmed her fingers over the rows of ribbons and medals one last time. I shrugged it off and draped it over my arm.

"You want me to go back to Houston instead?"

Jada's chin dropped. She bit her lower lip and delayed answering.

"Well?"

"I thought you'd go home after this was all said and done," she confessed. "Not because I want you to go home, but because you had your life back. I didn't think you'd pick up everything. Relocate your entire life."

"Jada, my life is with you, and your life is here. Your business. I'd never make you give that up.

"So what are you going to do about your shop in Houston?"

"Have my baby brother manage it." I grinned. "He's a bit of an idiot, but I think he can do it."

I took her by the hand and led the way upstairs. A brand new bedroom set had been the only new furniture purchase I'd made. Dark wood stood out against the cream walls and carpeted floor. My jacket found a new home atop the dresser, freeing my hands to slide up and down Jada's sides.

"You look beautiful tonight, Jada, but I think I wanna see you out of that dress."

She twisted around and bared the zipper to me. "Help me out?"

"Gladly." I tugged the zipper down, parting the royal-blue fabric until it slipped down and pooled at her ankles. My heart leapt at the sight of her, my soon-to-be-mate, clothed in a tightly laced corset and matching thong. I squeezed double handfuls of her plump ass and kneaded pliable flesh.

"I love when you wear these," I muttered.

Jada wore lace-top, black thigh-highs attached by garters to the corset. I imagined sliding her panties aside and fucking her in the skimpy lingerie.

"Unlace me?" With one coy glance over her shoulder, she filled me with feral lust and a raw desire to take charge. I plucked the knot loose then tucked my girl's body against me. Her ass perfectly framed my cock, both soft swells cradling it.

I growled and unfastened the front of her corset by memory, moving both hands over her curves to release the catches top to bottom. Both breasts spilled out as I dropped the restrictive device; then I cupped them and plucked the erect tips between my thumb and index finger.

"Tell me you want me, Jada. All of me."

"Taylor, you know I want you."

"No. All of me, Jada. I want… I want to claim you as my mate."

I released one tit and slid my hand down her subtle, soft tummy until I reached her panty line. Two fingers delved within after caressing smooth, completely waxed skin. Her pussy was so wet that one curving finger slid through her silky folds and into her body with ease.

"Did you think about it?" I asked when she only groaned a response.

"Y-yes," she stammered out, moving her hips, grinding. The tortuous movement placed pressure on my dick. "I talked with Dani and Leigh, too."

"What did they say?"

"That it'll be the best sex I've had in all of my life."

I chuckled against her ear then nipped the sensitive curve. "You think you can handle that?"

"Can you?" she countered, wriggling her ass against my hard cock.

I added a second digit, plunging in and out of her slickness, her body molding to me and clenching when I tweaked her nipple with the other hand. Jada's sassy teases faded into pleasured moans.

"It means we'll have a kid one day. Can you do that? Do you even *want* kids?"

Children were the one subject to never come up between us. Ever since I'd told her about my past with Sasha, she walked on eggshells regarding it.

"Taylor," she gasped out, moving and rolling her hips. "If you want a... yes, fuck, yes."

"It's not only about what I want, Jada. Do you want it?" I asked again, breathing against her ear, lips following her neck.

"Yes!"

It wasn't fair to tease her while discussing important subject matters, so I stopped. Both of my hands withdrew from her luscious curves, and then I stepped back to unfasten my pants. My hard dick strained for freedom until my boxers were around my ankles, balls so heavy and tight with the need for release that pre-cum glistened at the tip.

"Taylor?"

"Is this what you truly want, Jada?"

"I... do want kids. I've just never had a man I *wanted* to make a baby with. I'm not saying this to placate you." Jada's breaths remained quick but steady, her heaving chest causing both breasts to quiver enticingly. "I get it, Taylor. I didn't forget what you told me... this is like marriage."

I took her hand and kissed each of her knuckles while holding eye contact with her. "It is," I agreed. "I'll never love anyone the way I love you for the rest of my life."

"So... how do we do it?" Jada asked. "Do you bite me now or something like a werewolf movie?"

I stared at her.

"What? It's a legitimate question."

"You'll see." I chuckled despite the wave of goose bumps rising over my skin. "If I bite you, will you be upset with me?"

She shivered. "Is it necessary?"

"It may be." I stepped closer, bodies close enough to press my firm, rigid heat against her lower belly. "Once the mating bond starts, I won't be able to stop." I moved forward again, urging her back onto the bed without lowering myself to join her. I slipped her arms from around me and knelt, spreading her legs afterward to bare her sweet pussy.

Licking Jada was as much for my pleasure as it was for hers. I loved her taste, her smell, everything about the responsive way her body reacted to me. I was drunk on her, the worst kind of addict, and I lived for the way her brown eyes glazed over after orgasm. How she sighed my name while lying beside me in bed, drained of all energy and absolutely useless.

I started from the top, leaving no part of her neglected. Her mouth was a delicious treat, parting to accept the dart of my tongue between her lips while my busy hands traveled her curves. She sucked the tip of my tongue into her mouth playfully.

By the time I continued down, the tips of her breasts had pebbled tight. I nibbled one nipple then the next, their color as dark as cocoa and just as delectable. My tongue swirled over them in a time-consuming back and forth pattern, interrupted by the occasional scrape of my teeth, soothed only by another lick.

Once I kissed my way below her navel, I knew she'd never been wetter or more ready for my dick. I slipped two fingers into her to the knuckle.

"Fuck," I swore out loud, surprised by the moisture gathered by my exploring touch. She rocked her hips into the penetration, eager for more.

I responded by leaning down to lick her once, a tease before the main event. My tongue jostled the barbell through her delicate hood, prompting her to jerk and moan. Her toes curled as I traced her puffy folds with one finger. Then my lips closed around her clit, trapping the swollen nerve bundle for my tongue tip to flutter against it.

Two fingers plunged inside her, thrusting in and curving until I found her g-spot. She gasped out loud, raised her hips, and tried to rock against me in a desperate bid for orgasm. Adrenaline rushed through me, overwhelming my senses until it became a fight to remain selfless by bringing her to the first climax.

"Fuck, you're gorgeous," I breathed out, captivated by the sounds she made as I devoured her. I slid my finger down her pink slit again, parting her folds and denying her another penetration.

"Please!"

"Please what?" My words issued warm breath against her wet skin. She shuddered and writhed on the bed.

"I want you to… to…"

I wanted to hear her say the words, the seductive whisper of her requests always filling me with undeniable need.

"Taylor… I can't wait… I need it," she wailed out. "I need you inside me."

"Not until you come for me."

This time, when my lips closed around her tender button, I didn't stop until she squealed wildly and kicked with her legs. Her hips pumped, and then her mouth fell open in a soundless cry as her back arched against the sheets and her toes curled.

Without warning, I flipped Jada onto her belly and lowered atop her. One hand fisted my cock and directed the sensitive tip to her entrance, gliding my swollen crown through hot, wet folds. As I slipped between her glistening pussy lips, she inhaled a sharp breath.

A single stroke claimed her, and in doing so, I treated myself to a series of post-orgasm contractions. She clenched around me, hungry for my dick, spurring me to initiate a hard and reckless rhythm.

Sliding into her was like stealing my own little piece of heaven. Her pussy's tight embrace rippled in tiny post-climax aftershocks, inviting me to slam to the hilt and ride out her body's blissful reaction.

"Fuck," I groaned, gripping handfuls of her rounded ass. Her flesh was soft and pliant, jiggling beneath my hold. Without the presence of mind to speak anything else, I lapsed into silence. My feral instincts took over, my cougar demanding I finish what I started.

"Mine," I growled.

She liked it when I pulled her hair and fuck, so did I. I held a tight handful of her black waves in my left fist, and with my right, I brought my palm down against her cheek until it turned rosy and hot beneath my touch.

"Taylor!"

"Be mine, Jada."

Surrendering to the wild beast inside me, I thrust harder. Faster. Losing myself to the moment until nothing but her receptive grip mattered, hugging every inch of my thickness. The repetitious joining of our bodies created lewd slapping noises, wet skin to wet skin, my tight balls making methodic claps against her clit.

I bent down toward her neck. My lips were gentle at first, but the subsequent bite was not.

Startled, Jada cried out. I couldn't differentiate

pain from surprise, no more than I could stop and reign in my cougar.

"Say it, Jada. *Mine.*"

"Yours! I'm yours, Taylor!"

The tension burst at once, a blessed sensation of the ultimate relief. I released stream after stream of hot cum into her greedy sheath, only to grind against her at the end. The delicious trembles of our mutual climax milked me for the last spurt. Then I sagged against her.

$\sim$

JADA

"*B*e mine, Jada."

Something wild overcame my man. With the sheets clutched between my fingers, I held on to the bed for dear life while he pounded into me from behind. Instinctively, I grabbed at him, squeezing with my inner muscles while he plunged forward. In. Out. In. Clapping our bodies roughly together until the wet slurping noises competed with my fast and erratic breaths. Out. Making me feel painfully empty, stretched, and craving him again.

The tender press of his lips against my nape sent

a chain of tingles running down my spine, followed by a sharp flash of pain when his teeth clamped down on my sweat-glistened flesh. I cried out, pleasure and pain uniting as one indescribable sensation. I couldn't move, paralyzed by ecstasy as he plundered me.

"Say it, Jada. *Mine.*"

"Yours! I'm yours, Taylor!" I choked out, voice hoarse from my frantic gasps for air.

It was an explosion of sensation. A dizzying spiral that threatened to pull me under into oblivion. All I knew was Taylor's touch, his warmth as he filled me with his cum.

Everything I was, was his.

My legs gave out beneath me, and only Taylor's weight sagged down on my back kept me from sliding into a limp puddle on the floor. After a few moments, he dragged me further up the bed.

"Does this mean we're animal married?" I asked hazily.

Taylor chuckled at my question and tugged me closer, his skin hot against my sweaty body. My eyes drifted shut again as his fingers combed through my hair. "Like I said, it's the same thing as marriage to us. But..." He paused.

"But what?"

Taylor's weight left the bed. Curious, I rolled to

my side and propped up on one elbow, watching him. How he managed to walk straight without wobbling after sex was a mystery. He fetched something from his pants then climbed back into bed with me. A small, black velvet box was set down on my pillow.

All I could hear was the blood rushing through my head as my breath caught and my heart thudded hard in my chest. *Is it...? No, it couldn't be. But what if it is?*

Taylor opened the hinged lid and all the breath whooshed from my lungs.

It was a modest ring with a trio of small pink sapphires. Gorgeous, gold, and of the style I'd have picked for myself, proving he'd paid attention to my tastes in jewelry. I prized colorful and unique over expensive.

"Marry me, Jada. I know it hasn't been long, but being with you for the rest of my life is what I want to do. I'd know it even if my cougar hadn't chosen you, because I love you."

"Marry you?" My eyes burned with unshed tears. For the second time that day, I wept tears of joy. Before the wedding, I hadn't cried since putting Daddy to rest, but it felt damned good to cry again over something good. Over something he'd be proud of if he were still around.

"I know it's mostly a sheet of paper, but if it makes this more real for you—"

"You jackass, I don't need a sheet of paper for this to be real to me," I sobbed. Tears rolled freely down my cheeks, and I tried to wipe them away with the backs of my hands. "I love you. Yes."

I held out my left hand for Taylor to slide the ring onto my finger. It fit snugly, not too tight, but perfect, as if it had been measured.

Meant for me.

And they lived happily ever after...

The end

OTHER BOOKS BY PAYNE & TAYLOR

Epic Fantasy by Dominique Kristine

Shadows for a Princess

A princess who would rather die than wed. A warrior priest who would rather kill than see her harmed. A kingdom of shadows and treachery that threatens them both...

At the age of twenty-eight, Princess Ysolde Westbrook is a spinster duchess, the adopted daughter of Hindera's eccentric monarch. Commoners love their benevolent leader, but the kingdom's gentry take offense to the outsider among them. Amid noble plots and demands for her to marry a local aristocrat, an assassination attempt places her life in peril--if she will not have one of them for a husband, they would sooner see her dead.

Finding allies in strangers with powerful gifts and even darker secrets, Ysolde must learn what it means to lead and find her own inner strengths. Whether or not she survives the tangled web of treason will determine the fate of her duchy, the royal family, and the kingdom she loves.

Blend the intrigue of Game of Thrones with a touch of Outlander's romance for an adventurous fantasy in a whole new realm of magic. Fans of Diana Gabaldon and George R.R. Martin will love the richly descriptive world of Terraina.

ABOUT THE AUTHOR

Vivienne Savage is the pen name of two best friends who write everything together. One works as a nurse in a rural healthcare home in Texas, and the other is a U.S. Navy veteran. Both are mothers to two darling boys and two amazing girls.

All of their work varies in steam level, so pop by the VS website for details on which series is right for you!

For more information
www.viviennesavage.com
vivi@viviennesavage.com

www.ingramcontent.com/pod-product-compliance
Lightning Source LLC
Chambersburg PA
CBHW020326200626
46814CB00006BB/2438

* 9 7 8 1 9 4 6 4 6 8 1 5 4 *